LET US MAKE
GOD IN OUR IMAGE

B.J. Corey

Most Trafford titles are also available at major online book retailers.

Note for Librarians: A cataloguing record for this book is available from Library and Archives Canada at www.collectionscanada.ca/amicus/index-e.html

Printed in Victoria, BC, Canada.

ISBN: 978-1-4251-8624-1 (sc)

We at Trafford believe that it is the responsibility of us all, as both individuals and corporations, to make choices that are environmentally and socially sound. You, in turn, are supporting this responsible conduct each time you purchase a Trafford book, or make use of our publishing services. To find out how you are helping, please visit www.trafford.com/responsiblepublishing.html

Our mission is to efficiently provide the world's finest, most comprehensive book publishing service, enabling every author to experience success. To find out how to publish your book, your way, and have it available worldwide, visit us online at www.trafford.com

Trafford rev. 7/10/2009

Trafford
PUBLISHING® www.trafford.com

North America & international
toll-free: 1 888 232 4444 (USA & Canada)
phone: 250 383 6864 ♦ fax: 250 383 6804 ♦ email: info@trafford.com

The United Kingdom & Europe
phone: +44 (0)1865 487 395 ♦ local rate: 0845 230 9601
facsimile: +44 (0)1865 481 507 ♦ email: info.uk@trafford.com

FORWARD

Romans , chapter 1:

21. Because that, when they knew God, they glorified him not as God, neither were thankful; but became vain in their imaginations, and their foolish heart was darkened.

22. Professing themselves to be wise, they became fools,

23. And changed the glory of the uncorruptible God into an image made like to corruptible man, -----

25. Who changed the truth of God into a lie, and worshipped and served the creature more than the creator---

While the apostle Paul is speaking here in the past tense about attitudes and practices that were fairly common leading up to his time, it seems that such conduct has suddenly intensified at an alarming rate. While traditional Christianity is still alive and healthy, it seems that the other side has just recently launched a tremendous effort to spread confusion, disinformation, and doubt. The devil has gained a valuable ally in modern, enlightened, intellectual, secular mankind. I believe that down through the years, the devil has fabricated evidence that contradicts the biblical accounts of our origin and development, and modern man has willingly taken the bait. The devil would like nothing better than to convince the whole of mankind that there is no God, and while his fabrications and falsehoods are aimed at that goal, God will never let it come to fruition. The devil has, however, caused considerable doubt and unbelief in a goodly portion of society, and modern man of today seems to be a willing accomplice.

As a fundamentalist Christian, I am deeply concerned about the glut of misinformation about the Godhead of Father, Son, and Holy Ghost, and the holy Bible, that is being offered in the secular media today.

These offerings usually contradict the biblical accounts, and are based on rumor and innuendo. Their format is usually in the form of a documentary rather than a fictional piece, and the insinuation is there that they are based on historical facts, while most are not.

The frequency and brazenness of these "documentaries" of late is increasing at an alarming rate. It seems to me that mankind is trying to redefine God into someone that he can be comfortable with. If man can humanize God, bring God down to man's level then man does not have to rise to God's expectations. Modern mankind believes he has intellectually outgrown his former relationship with the God of the universe, no longer needs or desires his guidance, as in the original covenant, and has the audacity to presume that he can boldly renegotiate that covenant with God.

This book is an effort to counter the secular world's agenda and tell our side of the story, which I will be so bold as to say is God's side also.

While the television documentaries I mentioned are the main reason for writing this book, I decided early on to expand its scope to include other areas that are of concern to me. Thus this is a kind of "get it off your chest" thing. There, I feel better already!

Actually, the entire contents of this book have something to do with either man's attempt to deny God, to redefine God, or to redesign God, by all means at his disposal. While man's aspirations and nature may change often, God is the same, yesterday, today, and tomorrow. God never changes, nor does his covenant with mankind.

CHAPTER ONE

THE DIVINE NATURE OF SCRIPTURE

In order to fully understand who God is, one must first understand the nature and origin of the Bible.

The Bible consists of sixty six books, written by about half that many authors, over a period of a couple of thousand years. In view of the fact that these men wrote in different locations, at different times, and even in different languages, the possibility of there being any corroboration between them is practically nil.

Yet we see a marvelous harmony and continuity between the various writings that could only be brought about by some higher echelon of organization.

This is explained in II Timothy 3:16: *All scripture is given by inspiration of God----* It is my belief, as well as that of nearly all fundamental Christians, based on that verse, that these men were divinely and totally inspired by God. I believe that because God was in essence holding their hand, that they were incapable of any human error in their writings.

I would like to cite some examples. Old Testament prophets described upcoming events in vivid detail hundreds of years before their happenings. This is especially true concerning the birth of Jesus, his impact on the world, and his crucifixion.

There is no natural function of the human brain that allows one to foresee the future; therefore this function must be supernatural and come from some supernatural outside source. We call him God!

A perfect example of this can be found in the book of Isaiah which vividly describes the birth, ministry, and death of Christ. The findings of the Dead Sea scrolls in 1946, in a series of caves near Qumran on the Dead Sea completely validate the fact that the prophesies of Isaiah were written hundreds of years before the events occurred. Not only do they validate the book of Isaiah, but they validate nearly all the books of the Old Testament. Their authenticity is virtually unchallenged by both the religious and the secular world alike. They were discovered by a Bedouin goat tender named Muhammed Ahmed el-Hamed who, as a Muslim, would have absolutely no interest in fabricating such evidence, nor the capability to do so. The materials used in the scrolls, their condition upon discovery, and the clay jars they were contained in, definitely predate them to about the eighth or seventh century B.C., or approximately two thousand four hundred years before the King James Bible was published.

These scrolls also verify that through the years of copying, and translating into different languages, the original message of Isaiah remains unchanged, intact, and inerrant, a feat that strongly suggests divine oversight.

The prophet Isaiah wrote in 7:14: *Behold, a virgin shall conceive and bear a son and shall call his name Immanuel.*

Isaiah was born in 740BC so this prophesy must have been made at least 650 years before the advent of Christ's birth. While a virgin birth, by all medical standards is virtually impossible, why would a man of Isaiah's stature make such an unbelievable prediction? I can think of no other reason than that he was under the control of the Spirit of God at the time. The fact that the virgin birth did happen, bears this out.

The name Immanuel is also very significant as it means "God with us" in Hebrew. Isaiah was not only predicting the virgin birth, but he was predicting that Christ would literally be God in the flesh.

Let us look at another prediction by the prophet Isaiah in chapter 53:

6. All we like sheep have gone astray; we have turned every one to his own way; and the Lord hath laid on him the iniquity of us all.

7. He was oppressed, and he was afflicted, yet he opened not his mouth: he is brought as a lamb to the slaughter, and as a sheep before her shearers is dumb, so he openeth not his mouth.

8. He was taken from prison and from judgment; and who shall declare his generations? For he was cut off out of the land of the living: for the transgression of my people was he stricken.

9. And he made his grave with the wicked, and with the rich in his death; because he had done no violence, neither was any deceit in his mouth.

10. Yet it pleased the Lord to bruise him; he hath put him to grief: when thou shalt make his soul an offering for sin, he shall see his seed, he shall prolong his days, and the pleasure of the Lord shall prosper in his hand.

11. He shall see of the travail of his soul, and shall be satisfied: by his knowledge shall my righteous servant justify many: for he shall bear their iniquities.

12. Therefore will I divide him a portion with the great, and he shall divide the spoil with the strong; because he hath poured out his soul unto death; and he was numbered with the transgressors; and he bare the sins of many, and made intercession for the transgressors.

In verse six, *The Lord hath laid on him the iniquity of us all;* verse eight: *for the transgression of my people was he stricken;* verse eleven: *by his knowledge shall my righteous servant justify many: for he shall bear their iniquities;* these verses can only refer to Jesus Christ and no other.

Looking at this entire quote from Isaiah fifty three, it not only clearly identifies Jesus Christ as its subject, but it also clearly identifies the ministry of salvation that he would perform. *"The Lord hath laid on him the iniquity of us all."*

In verse eight we read: *"who will declare his generations? For he was cut off out of the land of the living."* It is evident to me that this not only speaks of his untimely death but also of the fact that he had no natural offspring to carry on the family name, contrary to what is presently being libelously suggested by the modern media. Now if we look in verse ten we read: *"when thou shalt make his soul an offering for sin, he shall see his seed"* does that not clearly describe the New Testament practice of accepting Christ as one's savior? The souls that are redeemed by his shed blood are the seed that "he shall see". Remember that this was written six hundred and fifty years before the birth of Christ! Where could the prophet Isaiah have received the wisdom to describe the life and ministry of Jesus with such clarity? Divine inspiration seems to be the only answer!

5

There is something quite remarkable about verses eleven and twelve in that God is speaking through the prophet Isaiah, BUT HE IS SPEAKING IN THE FIRST PERSON!

It is extremely improbable that Isaiah would refer to Christ as my righteous servant, (verse 11), and in verse 12, only God would have the authority to divide him a portion with the great.

This fact that God is speaking in the first person should be adequate proof of divine inspiration.   But, there is more.   We will now look at the amazing harmony in what Isaiah wrote, and the New Testament apostles recorded.

With all these prophesies of Isaiah in mind, let us turn to Mathew, chapter one:

18. Now the birth of Jesus Christ was on this wise: When as his mother Mary was espoused to Joseph, before they came together, she was found with child of the Holy Ghost.

19. Then Joseph her husband, being a just man, and not willing to make her a publick example was minded to put her away privily

20. But while he thought on these things, behold, the angel of the Lord appeared unto him in a dream, saying, Joseph, thou son of David, fear not to take unto thee Mary thy wife: for that which is conceived in her is of the Holy Ghost.

Now let us go to the gospel of Luke, chapter one:

26. And in the sixth month the angel Gabriel was sent from God unto a city of Galilee, named Nazareth.

27. To a virgin espoused to a man whose name was Joseph, of the house of David; and the virgin's name was Mary.

28. And the angel came in unto her and said, hail thou that art highly favored, the Lord is with thee: blessed art thou among women.

29. And when she saw him, she was troubled at his saying, and cast in her mind what manner of salutation this should be.

30. And the angel said unto her, fear not Mary, for thou hast found favour with God.

31. And behold, thou shalt conceive in thy womb, and bring forth a son, and shalt call his name JESUS.

32. He shall be great, and shall be called the son of the Highest; and the Lord God shall give unto him the throne of his father David.

33. And he shall reign over the house of Jacob for ever; and of his kingdom there shall be no end.

34. Then said Mary unto the angel, how shall this be, seeing I know not a man?

35. And the angel answered and said unto her, The Holy Ghost shall come upon thee, and the power of the Highest shall overshadow thee; therefore also that holy thing that shall be born of thee shall be called the Son of God.

Considering the selected verses that we have just read, we can readily see a distinct harmony between the writings of Isaiah, Mathew, and Luke. This harmony could not be present to this degree without a single force directing it. Going back to II Timothy: *All scripture is given by inspiration of God---.*

Whether or not you believe in divine inspiration at this point does not really change the facts. For these writings to be a hoax, (something I vehemently deny) there still had to be one single organizer who lived more than 650 years, and convinced Isaiah, Mathew, Luke, Joseph, Mary, and later Jesus himself to all be on the same sheet of music. Quite a feat, don't you think? That talented person should make the Guinness book of records. (Don't bother to look)!

Another example of the harmony in scripture can be found in Psalm 22, better known as the crucifixion Psalm. It was written by David hundreds of years before the crucifixion of Christ. While crucifixion was not even practiced in David's day, this psalm vividly describes the unique pain and suffering of a crucifixion.

1. My God, my God, why hast thou forsaken me? Why art thou so far from helping me, and from the words of my roaring?

2. Oh my God, I cry in the daytime, but thou hearest not; and in the night season, and am not silent.

3. But thou art holy, oh thou that inhabitest the praises of Israel.

4. Our fathers trusted in thee: they trusted, and thou didst deliver them.

5. They cried unto thee, and were delivered: they trusted in thee, and were not confounded.

6. But I am a worm, and no man; a reproach of men and despised of the people.

7. All they that see me laugh me to scorn: they shoot out the lip, they shake the head, saying,

8. He trusted on the Lord that he would deliver him: let him deliver him, seeing that he delighted in him.

9. But thou art he that took me out of the womb: thou didst make me hope when I was upon my mothers breasts.

10. I was cast upon thee from the womb: thou art my God from my mother's belly.

11. Be not far from me; for trouble is near; for there is none to help.

12. Many bulls have compassed me: strong bulls of Bashan have beset me round.

13. They gaped upon me with their mouths, as a ravening and a roaring lion.

14. I am poured out like water, and all my bones are out of joint: my heart is like wax; it is melted in the midst of my bowels.

15. My strength is dried up like a potsherd; and my tongue cleaveth to my jaws; and thou hast brought me into the dust of death.

16. For dogs have compassed me; the assembly of the wicked have inclosed me: they pierced my hands and my feet.

17. I may tell all my bones: they look and stare upon me.

18. They part my garments among them, and cast lots for my vesture.

I can only assume that David's vivid description is a revelation from God. David could not possibly have been describing a revelation of his own death, for he died peaceably at home, presumably in bed. (I Kings, ch 2). Also verses fourteen, fifteen, and sixteen, are a fairly accurate description of the suffering of the act of crucifixion, a form of punishment invented by the Persians long after David wrote the Psalm.

There are two verses that point to the fact that it specifically describes the crucifixion of Jesus. First, in verse one it starts with the words: *My God, My God, why hast thou forsaken me.* These are the exact words, verbatim, that Jesus uttered while on the cross, at the moment when he willfully accepted the guilt for all the sins of mankind. At that point, the Father, who could not abide with sin, turned his back on Jesus.

The second verse I want to point out is verse 18: *They part my garments among them, and cast lots for my vesture.*

The Roman soldiers who crucified Jesus did exactly that and it is recorded in all four Gospels.   Mathew 27:35; Mark 15:24; Luke 23:24; and John 19:24.

There are numerous other examples of Old Testament prophesies that were fulfilled to the letter in the New Testament and most moderately priced Bibles have a section in the back that lists all of them.

I believe that I have covered enough territory to establish the premise that the original writings were divinely inspired by God himself, but what about the copies, of copies, of translations, that we use today?   Some liberal Bible scholars have espoused the idea that during the process of copying and translating into different languages over the years that the original writings have probably become tainted to some degree.   They are taking God out of the picture.   I have also heard critics say that some Hebrew or Greek words have no counterpart in the English language.   God knows that.   When the original manuscripts were written He was there, when the translators were doing their work, He was there,   When the specific Bible that I use daily was in the process of printing, He was there.   My Bible is a direct gift from God, and I treat it as though He were speaking directly to me.

When God gave these scriptures to mankind, he conveyed a specific message that he intended to be eternal.   If he was capable of divinely inspiring the original writers, is he not also capable of maintaining this eternal specificity?   In the book of Revelations God gives a warning to mankind to neither take away any portion of this book or to add to any portion.   He offers dire consequences for such actions.   Some people are of the opinion that this warning applies only to the book of Revelations, but I believe it applies to the whole Bible.

To consider that man had any input into the message of the Bible, as is being suggested today,   is to render Christian religion ineffective as an absolute truth, and opening the door to inaccurate and varying speculations of the character and nature of God.   This is being done increasingly today. Knowing the importance that God placed on the Bible, I am certain that He was present in every aspect of its origin, its development, and its distribution.   As God is aware of every single moment of the future, He knew before hand what its impact would be on mankind, and He would allow nothing less than divine perfection in its message.

Its message is forthright and easily understood by an open mind. The often heard complaint that it is hard to understand is usually just an excuse for not accepting its directions. Some of the same people who claim the Bible is hard to understand will read William Shakespeare and extol the complexity of his writings.

You may call me narrow minded, for I not only favor the King James version of the Bible, but it is the only one on the market today that I can be sure is divinely inspired. For hundreds of years the King James has been the only Bible used by clergy and laity alike. Only within the last three or four decades did all the modern day versions gain significant popularity. I have examined some of these newer versions, comparing them to the King James, and they do not merely simplify the language, but in many key verses the meaning is radically altered. Why? I can only assume that it is part of man's desire to not only redefine God, but also his message to mankind. Is it merely coincidence that these modern versions show up about the same time that mankind developed a desire to redesign God? Methinks there may be a correlation there!

The Bible is the most prominent evangelical tool available to mankind, and the devil has tried for centuries to discredit it by spreading misinformation. The secular media of today has innocently become a willing ally, bombarding the inter-net and the airways with alternate "exposé's" of God's message. Their purpose seems to be to reinterpret the Bible, and redefine God.

In short, the only true revelation of the personality, character, and purpose of God, is contained in the Holy Bible, of which He is the sole author. Today's deviations from, and abstract interpretations of, its teachings, have no basis in fact or even theory, and are delusions of the human mind, or concoctions of the devil, designed to modify or redefine the image of God.

My grandma used to have a saying: "the same old gospel that once saved me, is the same old gospel that'll set you free". I like to put it this way: if it ain't broke, don't fix it!

CHAPTER TWO

EVOLUTION OR INTELLIGENT DESIGN?

First off, I have a little problem with the term intelligent design. I believe that term is a compromise meant to appease the evolutionists, and a much more definitive term would be divine design. All the religions of the world who believe in intelligent design, attribute creation to a deity, therefore the term divine design seems more appropriate.

Evolution and divine design, when analyzed from a purely scientific standpoint, are classified as theories. In other words, there is no direct evidence to support them as facts. A theory is derived from analysis of a certain set of circumstances and carrying them out to their most logical conclusion when no direct evidence is available.

Due to the fact that these two theories are so directly opposed to one another, only one can possibly be the most logical, the other must be discarded as worthless. Because of the vast difference between the two groups of circumstantial evidence that support these theories, one group must, at least in part, be fabricated. I submit that the devil is completely capable of fabricating the evidence to support the theory of evolution, and I further accuse him of doing just that to some degree. He cannot provide definite proof, because God will not allow him to go that far.

The theory of divine design was first to come on the scene, and has been around ever since man was created. Beginning with Adam, man had knowledge of God as creator.

The theory of evolution came later. From its onset its proponents denied the concept of creation by God in their conclusions. They put forth the theory that trillions upon trillions of singular, natural events occurred in the proper order to elevate the universe from utter chaos to what it is today. This number of events is astronomical, and most probably so large as to be immeasurable, even with today's mega-computers. To assume that all of these events occurred haphazardly, in order, with no prior plan, and no choreography, is the height of absurdity!

Just to demonstrate how absurd their premise is, take the average two hole kitchen toaster, a fairly simple machine, disassemble it into it's several parts, and place those parts haphazardly into a canvas bag. Shake it up, kick it across the room, drop it on the floor several times, cool it, heat it, soak it, dry it, in short, apply any type force you desire to this sack of parts, then look into the bag and see if it has reassembled itself into a toaster. Keep repeating the process until it comes out right. Sounds totally absurd doesn't it? The parts represent the components of the universe, the shaking, kicking, dropping or whatever, represent the dynamic forces that they assume acted on these components to create what we have today.

While I cannot be absolutely certain, I suspect that at least some of these men were more interested in removing God from the recipe, than in furthering the knowledge of science, and that many of their conclusions were biased by that prime objective.

As their theory developed, they came up against a brick wall. One of the basic laws of science is this: matter can neither be created nor destroyed. If the current life forms did evolve as they suggest, then where did the matter they evolved from come from? They simply came up with another theory. In order to solve this quandary, they came up with the "big bang" theory to explain the origin of matter. Evolution now becomes a theory based on a theory.

But wait a minute, for the big bang to occur as they suggest, wouldn't that require some ultra-dynamic mega-force? And where did this mega-force come from? We can carry this line of reasoning on into infinity, but the only logical conclusion would be that there has to be something or someone eternal and supernatural. As Christians, we identify this eternal supernatural force as God, and we believe in the biblical account of our world's origin.

Eternity is a concept that is all but impossible for the human analytical mind to comprehend. Nearly all scientific principles are described by measurements such as time, space, and distance, but eternity has none of the above. It is almost like a fifth dimension with absolutely no boundaries. I can neither explain, describe, nor understand it but I know that for me to exist as a clump of matter there must be a concept of eternity.

How did life begin? Evolutionists theorize that life began as a simple one cell life form that evolved over billions of years into today's complex forms. I watched a program on television recently where a Christian professor of math explained the possibility of this happening. The odds against it were so enormous that only with today's super computers could they be calculated. I wish I had written his figures down, but at the time, I had no idea that I would one day be writing this book. I was so awe-struck by this man's explanation though, that I will never forget the basic structure of his presentation. He began by saying that this one celled creature would be made up of several kinds of amino acids and proteins. It would be made up of a chain of groups of these components, and here is where my memory fails me to a degree. The chain had to consist of either fifteen groups of four components each, or fourteen groups of five each, I don't remember which, and it may have been neither, but those figures are definitely very close to his presentation.. What made the odds so great is the fact that each of these individual components had to be in its proper place in the group, and each group had to be in its proper place in the chain. The odds of this happening were one in ten to the 1640th power or one in ten to the 1460th power, I don't remember which. Even using the smallest figure that is ten with 1460 zeroes behind it! Just to give you an idea of how large a number we are talking about, I timed myself, and I discovered that I could write seventy zeroes in one minute. That means it would take a little over twenty minutes just to write the number, if you didn't get writer's cramp first. The odds of you winning the lottery are probably a million times greater than the odds of this one celled creature haphazardly developing! While I retrieved these figures from a seventy year old cranial data base (my brain), after they had rattled around in there for some ten or fifteen years, I can say for sure that the end result was one in ten to the one thousandth plus power. Does it seem logical to base a theory on such improbability? Give me the Bible account any day!

An enormous disparity exists in the time line offered by evolutionists, and the time line offered in the biblical account of creation. The Bible states that God created the earth and all that is in it in a six day period, while evolutionists say it took billions of years.

An evolutionist once argued with me that I couldn't possibly be right in believing the biblical account because according to the Bible the earth is only six thousand years old, and science has evidence that it is billions of years old.

Do they? Are we talking about the same people who once thought the sun revolved around the earth? Who once believed the earth was flat? Who revised their carbon dating process each time they discovered a discrepancy between its results and known history? I have about as much faith in their carbon dating process as I have in Ford Motor Company reviving the Edsel. Scientists begrudgingly admit that there are some immeasurable variables that affected the carbon molecules during their aging process, and while carbon dating is a valuable tool in cataloguing relics in a chronological sequence, its accuracy in determining the age of a particular specimen has proved to be wrong in the past.

Some liberal Christians, as well as some Christian scientists, try to combine the two theories by suggesting that each creative day covered millions of years. They may be reading their Bible but they don't get the picture! In Genesis 1:5 we read: *and the evening and the morning were the first day.* Going on to verse eight: *and the evening and the morning were the second day.* I see two distinct things in these passages that they apparently overlook. First He says and the evening and the morning on each consecutive day, that to me represents one twenty four hour day, and secondly, going back to my days in the first grade when I learned to count, doesn't second immediately follow first? Sometimes trying to combine science with the Bible is kind of like eating catsup on ice cream!

Another discrepancy that I see in their theory's time line is the long term effect on the atmosphere. They would have us believe that the plant life came first, and millions of years later, animal life came into being. Way back in fifth or sixth grade science class, I learned that plants depended heavily for the propagation of their species on animal activity for the distribution of seeds and pollination. If there were no animals, no bees, no hummingbirds, then what provided this service for the plants?

In science class, I also learned that plants take in carbon dioxide and through photosynthesis, produce oxygen, while animals take in oxygen, giving off carbon dioxide. If there were no animals for millions of years, where did the plants get their carbon dioxide from? Evolutionists would probably argue that there was a lot more volcanic activity back then and that produced the carbon dioxide, a theory I accept reluctantly with some measure of doubt. Even if this were true, on day one of that period of millions of years, the plants would begin to produce oxygen. As there was little or no consumption of that oxygen, the atmosphere would become more and more oxygenated. As the oxygen content became greater there would of necessity be a decrease in the other gasses, including carbon dioxide. Also, the volcanic activity during that period would gradually taper off some-what, creating less and less carbon dioxide. I have my doubts that plant life could survive through the period that they claim.

Another problem I suspect in an increasingly oxygenated atmosphere is that the increasing oxygen content combined with the rotting vegetation and the heat of the volcanic activity would eventually result in the earth becoming a self destructing mega-bomb.

To me, it seems much more logical to believe that God created plant life on creative day three, and animal life on days five and six, as He recorded in Genesis chapter one.

Not being a scientist, or having a desire to be one, I will readily admit that some of the thoughts I have recorded in this chapter concerning the plant life and its carbon dioxide supply are based on conjecture on my part, but if they can speculate, so can I. My only hope is that I have given you some food for thought.

Evolutionists point to the fossil trail as evidence to back up their theory. They have brainwashed the majority of mankind into believing that there is only one "missing link" to be discovered and the trail will be complete. What they actually have is bits and pieces with gaps in between. Using their premise that all species living today have one origin, then one would have to surmise that every specie, with the exception of that first life form, evolved from some lower specie. There should then be fossil evidence to support that evolution all the way from amoeba to man. It would seem to me that after all the interest, effort, time, and resources that have been expended to date, that science would have developed this fossil trail to the extent that evolution could be proved to be a fact rather than just a theory. If such evidence existed, it would be the researchers "holy grail", and they would profoundly publicize its existence. They haven't because it doesn't exist.

In 1984, an author named Luther Sunderland wrote a book entitled: *Darwin's Enigma: Fossils and Other Problems.* In it he recounts interviews with the curators of five separate museums which had extensive fossil collections, (over 250,000 items total) in the five museums. He states that every one of the five admitted that there was no fossil evidence to support the evolutionist's theory. I suspect that at least a majority of these men, if not all, were sympathetic to the theory of evolution due to their positions, yet they could not validate it.

In the biblical account of creation in the book of Genesis, God says that he made every animal "after his kind". I submit that the very first cow that God made bore a remarkable resemblance to the bovines of today, and there is no fossil evidence that the cow evolved from any other creature.

In their zeal to support their theory, some researchers have taken some small clue, and by assuming much, turned it into what they term a major discovery. One such case was a small isolated bone found during a "dig" in the Midwest, before DNA testing became available. It was hailed as a rare find, part of some animal that supposedly lived millions of years ago. Years later, upon DNA testing, it turned out to be part of your everyday barnyard hog!

Mentally, man is by far the most highly developed creature on the planet, while physically, he is much weaker than nearly all the carnivores, even those of equal, or slightly lesser size. Why then do these carnivores hunt and kill prey that is much harder to acquire than man would be, and leave man alone? The answer can be found in Genesis chapter one, verse twenty eight.

And God blessed them, (Adam and Eve) and God said unto them, be fruitful, and multiply, and replenish the earth, and subdue it: and have dominion over the fish of the sea, and over the fowl of the air, and over every living thing that moveth upon the earth.

While the word psyche applies to the human mind, for lack of a better word, I submit that God instilled in the psyche of each animal that they were to be subjective to mankind. While there are accounts of occasional animal attacks on humans, these animals for the most part treat man with a reverence and awe that they do not afford to any other specie. Whenever these attacks occur, it is usually because the humans provoked them. If it were not for the enforcement by God of man's dominion over creation, the carnivores of the planet should have easily annihilated man in the beginning stages of his development, especially if, as the evolutionists claim, he began as an illiterate cave dweller.

Some years ago I began to raise and train horses. (Every self respecting Texan must do this at least once in their lifetime.) While working with a two year old stallion, I began to ponder the relationship between myself and this fine, high spirited beast. I came to the conclusion that this animal could snuff out my life in an instant if he cared to, yet he endured my novice efforts to teach him to do things that were unnatural behavior to him. We actually developed a bond, where he had a strong desire to please me. As I marveled at this relationship, I realized that this was all part of God's intention that man should have dominion over all creation. I wonder if the horse didn't teach me more than I taught him.

Now as to man's intelligence. Why is there such a large gap between the intelligence of man and the intelligence of all lower species? While for every other specie, one can find another specie that is similar in intelligence all the way from the dolphin down to the lowly earthworm, but there is a huge gap between the smartest animal and mankind. In other words, if the intelligence of all the creatures were placed on a grade scale, there would be a gradual increase in intelligence beginning with the simplest forms of life until you reach the most complex, and then a tremendous gap between the most complex of creatures and mankind. If man evolved from a squatting, grunting, creature that sometimes walked on all fours, why did not the causes that affected his intelligence also have a similar effect on at least some of the other species? We know that man has been conversing intelligently for at least six thousand years. If man's capability to speak gradually evolved as they claim, it would seem that by now, there ought to be a similar evolution in the speech capabilities of some of the animals. (Pardon me, I forgot about Mr. Ed, the talking horse on TV!) But seriously, while science has discovered that nearly all species have some method of communicating within the specie, these methods at best are rudimentary, and there is no evidence of their improving in any way. The need and the desire to communicate are primal. Shouldn't the other creatures be evolving too? In a couple of thousand years will visitors to the Paris zoo be able to listen to the polar bears speak French? I think not.

I submit that man's intelligence was always there, given to him by God in the Garden of Eden.

I have a steadfast belief in divine creation. This belief is not based solely on any circumstantial evidence, (although there is an ample quantity of such evidence if one is to look with an open mind), this belief is based on absolute faith. Through my intimate relationship of the last twenty seven years with God's word, I have developed a complete trust in its accuracy, its completeness, and its divine authorship. Only those who are unfamiliar with it can doubt its authenticity.

When analyzed through the eyes of modern secular man, it would seem that the two theories should be about even in their believability, yet evolution has been taught in our schools as near fact for years, while divine creation has been shunned, and in most cases banned from mere mention.

While I reluctantly agree that to credit the God of the Bible exclusively for creation, (to me, a biblical fact), approaches unconstitutionality under the freedom of religion clause, (more about this later) teaching divine creation by an unnamed deity would not. I would even settle for their moniker of "Intelligent design". To teach intelligent design as a theory, giving it equal credence with the theory of evolution, could not in your wildest dreams be considered as religious education. Then why is it not being done? Because the critics know that if man is taught that some higher power may have been involved, he will soon put two and two together, and realize that the Bible account seems extremely plausible. The dedicated fanatical efforts by some special interest groups to prohibit this from happening can only be motivated by a strong desire to eliminate God from the conscience of man. But not to worry, for one day you'll meet him! (On second thought, maybe a little worry is appropriate.)

CHAPTER THREE

SENSATIONALISM IN THE CHURCH

Why is this misinformation so popular today? Mankind seems to have developed an insatiable thirst for religious sensationalism.

This thirst actually began back in the social rebellion of the sixties. Higher institutions of learning which had long been the bulwark of the status quo converted to liberal thinking and thousands of students took to the streets in protest rallies.

The war in Viet-Nam may have been the catalyst, but there was a far deeper reason for their unrest. They wanted to develop a society with little or no restrictions, where most anything was lawful, and each member was responsible for developing his or her own moral code. The moral code that was believed by most of society to have been divinely instituted by God, was passé to their thinking and far too definitive. They wanted a substitute code that was vague, and would allow for excursions in to heretofore inappropriate behavior without repercussions.

In the book of Isaiah, chapter one, we read: *17. Learn to do well,, seek judgment, relieve the oppressed, judge the fatherless, plead for the widow.*

18. Come now, and let us reason together, saith the Lord: though your sins be as scarlet, they shall be as white as snow; though they be red like crimson, they shall be as wool.

19. If ye be willing and obedient, ye shall eat the good of the land:

20. But if ye refuse and rebel, ye shall be devoured with the sword, for the mouth of the Lord hath spoken it.

God says, come let us reason together, today's man wants to "reason" within himself, leaving God out of the picture. It really doesn't matter that mankind has redefined the moral code, it wasn't his option; it wasn't his code.   God has promised severe punishment for his actions.

Remember the phrase "anti-establishment"?   The dreaded establishment that they were so dissatisfied with was the system of democratic free enterprise capitalism that by its very nature provided them with the means and the freedom to revolt against it! This system was deeply rooted in the Judeo-Christian ethic, and its founders were for the most part deeply religious men.

These protesters embraced socialism because it was the anti-thesis of capitalism and by its nature, denied the authority of God. As a glaring example of this, during the reign of Nikita Kruschev, a high ranking member of the Russian politburo said in a public speech: "In due course, we will meet God on his terms, and defeat him."

Capitalism endorsed a moral code that was clearly defined and somewhat restrictive.   These restrictions were based on the biblical accounts of acceptable behavior that had passed the test of time, and were accepted by the majority of mankind as the way he ought to behave.

These radical free thinkers decided to step "out of the box" and devise a whole new set of rules in the guise of free expression. They wanted God out of the picture, or at least redefined.   Their experimentation had disastrous results.

The liberal socialist attitude of the sixties spilled over into the church, and fostered a desire for alternatives to traditional religion. This culminated in debacles like the Mooneys, the Jim Jones Jonestown tragedy, and the Branch Davidians in Waco Texas, to name a few. This was sensationalism at its ugliest.

As a young man growing up in rural Vermont, I recall there were basically only three church denominations anywhere in the state. These were the Catholic church, the Baptist church, and the Congregationalist church, (a branch of Methodist).   Now on every other street corner you can find a "stand alone" church with a catchy name.   This church in most cases developed not out of a community need, but out of one man's desire to foster his own peculiar doctrines.   The more sensational the message, the more radical the doctrines, the more popular the church.

For those who never attend church, there is the electronic media. Instead of dressing up, getting the kids ready, cleaning the car, etc. we can just stay home and watch reverend Humpty Dumpty on channel seven. We like him a lot better than reverend Howdy Do on channel nine. Does that sound familiar? Don't get me wrong, I am not against the "electronic church", In fact, I have been on both sides of the fence, having conducted a radio ministry for several years, but I am dead set against it becoming an alternative to attendance in a local body. In the book of Hebrews God says: *Forsake not the assembling of your-selves, as is the manner of some---".* There are two main functions of the local church. Organized worship and organized evangelism, each requiring an adequate number of warm bodies to accomplish these tasks!

The local church also needs financial support in order to minister to those in need as they are called to do by God. If a goodly number of the Christians in the community of the local church send their tithes to media ministries, then the church must struggle just to pay its monthly bills and there will be nothing left to minister to the needy. While it may not be their intent, these media ministries conduct a vigorous campaign to solicit operating funds that often siphons off money that should have been donated to the local church. I am not advocating non-support for the media ministries, but I am a firm believer that God expects us to pay our tithes to the local church, and then if we are financially able, to support the media ministries. While we are on this subject, have you ever noticed some of the ultra-elaborate and very expensive studio settings of some of these media outlets that are provided by our gifts?

The electronic church is not necessarily by design, but certainly by its nature, in direct competition with local churches. Maybe they could go off the air from 9:30 till 12:00 on Sunday morning, signing off with an earnest plea for their viewers to go to church. (Just a thought).

The electronic church does provide a valuable ministry to the sick and shut in, and those who physically cannot attend church due to travel or work requirements, but that should be its only function.

In my estimation, the electronic church of today has become more entrepreneurial than evangelical. There are some exceptions, but these seem to be in the minority. Many of these programs bolster their support base with special offers of medallions, lapel pins, statues, recorded materials, literature, cut rate trips to the Holy Land, Etc. This is not only sensationalism, but it is merchandising God. Do you remember why Jesus made a whip and cleansed the Temple?

Another form of sensationalism that is popping up frequently is the preacher that has discovered some radical new secret that was heretofore deeply hidden in the Holy Scriptures, just waiting for him to come on the scene, and announce it to the world. It is totally absurd to think that God was hiding this tidbit of information all these years, but this man was the only one smart enough to discover God's hiding place. First, God does not hide any part of his message that he intends mankind to have, and secondly, if God were to hide it, no man would be smart enough to discover it! There are hundreds of cult religions today that were started by just such men, based on their own abstract interpretation of some minute portion of scripture. The Branch Davidians and David Koresh immediately come to mind.

We also have the preacher that feels he has to compete with his peers. He feels he must go one better than the competition. I have seen this attitude displayed at area fellowships, and between pastors when there is more than one church of their denomination in town. While it only happens on occasion, it shouldn't happen at all. God expects cooperation, not competition.

I believe these faulty preachers are a product of a very relaxed ordination process. The church has relaxed its standards, (or should I say God's standards?), to the point where nearly anyone can be ordained today. I personally know two individuals who purchased their ordination certificates through the mail! There are gay preachers, women preachers, and preachers whose children are hers, mine, and ours, (divorced and remarried). Now I know that statement right there will most probably anger a lot of folks, but don't even bother to contact me for an apology, I ain't a gonna do it! (Texas lingo comes out sometimes.)

God has always maintained stricter standards for the clergy than for the layman. A good example of this is King David, of whom God said, was "a man after my own heart." Yet, when David expressed a desire to build God's temple in Jerusalem, God told him: "no, David, you have blood on your hands." God was not speaking of the blood David had shed in his many battles at God's direction, but the blood of Uriah the Hittite. David arranged to have Uriah killed in battle so that he could take his wife Bathsheba. Because of that sin, God considered David not pure enough to build his temple, although He let David remain as king of Israel.

In the book of I Samuel, we find the story of Phinehas and Hophni, two brothers who were sons of the priest, Eli. They assumed special importance for themselves because their father was the priest, and took advantage of their position. They demanded sexual favors from the women who ministered in the temple, and their final act was to offer up incense to the Lord when it was not required of them, neither was it their responsibility. For those acts, God took both their lives, and then called Samuel to be the priest in place of Eli's sons because Eli failed to control his children. (Preacher beware!)

We can see from these Old Testament stories that God has always held his chosen rulers and the clergy to exemplary standards. The New Testament standards are no different, although many today sometimes choose to ignore them.

In I Timothy, chapter 3:

1. This is a true saying, if a man desires the office of a bishop, (pastor) he *desireth a good work*

2. A bishop then must be blameless the husband of one wife, vigilant, sober, of good behavior, given to hospitality, apt to teach;

3. not given to wine, no striker, not greedy of filthy lucre, but patient, not a brawler, not covetous;

4. One that ruleth well his own house, having his children in subjection with all gravity;

5. for if a man know not how to rule his own house, how shall he take care of the church of God?

6. Not a novice lest being lifted up with pride he fall into the condemnation of the devil.

7. Moreover he must have a good report of them which are without; lest he fall into reproach and the snare of the devil.

These requirements seem to be taken very nonchalantly today by some ministering pastors and by most church ordination councils. Church ordination councils have become a mere formality where the candidate is coached before hand to the extent that he knows the questions and answers before going into the examination. This was my own experience in 1987 when I was ordained. I know that my pastor meant well, but my ordination was confirmed before I even entered the sanctuary. If one can memorize eight or nine Bible passages, (most pre-school Sunday schoolers can do this), he is usually a shoo-in. I have known old timey preachers who have told me they went before ordaining councils two or three times before being accepted. In the past, a candidate was usually licensed to preach first, and then after a certain period of intense scrutiny, a decision was made whether to ordain him. Not all licensed preachers were ordained.

I look very skeptically upon pastorates that are passed down from father to son. I believe more pastors today are called by Mom & Pop, or by the church congregation than by the Lord. I have three sons, and I would never encourage them to become preachers unless I was certain that they were called of God. Quite to the contrary, I would try my best to discourage them, knowing that if they were truly called of God; my attempts to discourage them would fall on deaf ears. There is a natural tendency for the farmer to want his son to be a farmer, for the butcher to want his son to be a butcher, but preachers are selected by God, not family succession. Ordination is not something that one seeks, but is something one is called of God to do. Ordination requires a total separation to a Godly life to the utmost degree.

Quite a large number of pastors today have been married more than once. In my lifetime, there has always been a lot of controversy about what "*the husband of one wife*" means in first Timothy, chapter two, and verse three. This verse can be interpreted in a number of ways, and it certainly has been over the years, especially of late. The generally accepted majority opinion has always been that divorce and remarriage disqualifies one from being a pastor. It could also be said that divorce and remarriage is a failure to comply with the requirement in verses four and five to "*rule well his own house*". It amazes me how many men have held to that majority opinion at first, and immediately revised their interpretation once they themselves were divorced and remarried!

It seems to me that there are more and more pastors today who consider their calling a "nine to five" profession. When being interviewed for a position in a church, their main concern is how much do I get paid, what are the fringe benefits, and how much vacation do I get, when their only concern should be has God called me to be here. If God called you to be there, he will take care of you!

While we are on that subject, a congregation should always take care of its pastor! There should never be a pastor who has to hold down a secular job on the side to take care of his family. He should be free every day to minister to the needs of his flock. Over half of the pastors that I know at present have jobs in the secular world. In over half of these cases I believe that if each of their church members tithed as they should, that the church would be capable of giving their pastor a full time salary.

I don't want anyone to get the idea that I have a "Holier than thou" attitude about this. As I write this, God is very adamantly convicting me of my own shortcomings as a minister of his gospel. At this point, I feel a strong desire to stop what I am doing, kneel in prayer, and beg his forgiveness. Excuse me for a moment.

CHAPTER FOUR

THE GOD OF THE MEDIA

The protesters we mentioned in the previous chapter have grown up now, and have to make a living. Not wanting to be part of evil, greedy, corporate America, they have settled down in three areas where they can still spread their propaganda, the media, the movies, and our educational system. In this chapter we will deal with the media.

As an avid fan of history, I like to watch the information channels on the TV. Of late, there have been an increasing number of so called documentaries concerning the life and ministry of Jesus, and the origin, purpose and content of the Bible. These are usually narrated by one or more "experts" with lofty titles from some university but seldom do I see the title Dr. of divinity. They are professors of mideast studies, or professors of anthropology, or professors of history Etc. I believe the reason you never see a Dr. of divinity is that any real man of God would have nothing to do with their wild tales. In my estimation, going to these so called experts to learn of God, would be about the same as going to the taxi stand and asking the dispatcher to explain some facet of brain surgery.

While I cannot say with a surety that these networks and producers have any hidden agenda, there does seem to be a concerted effort on the part of some to discredit traditional Christian beliefs. I do know that many of these producers and net-work executives came out of the sixties anti-establishment movement.

To be fair, they frequently offer the Bible explanation of the material they are presenting, but they almost always counter with an alternative based on rumor or innuendo, sometimes on vague scientific theories. The material is presented in such a way that the alternative explanation usually carries the most weight, thus making it easy for the viewer to believe the biblical account to be fable, and the alternative to be probable fact. Repetition of this ploy in one documentary after another, could easily lead one to believe that the whole Bible is fable.

In order to determine the effect of these programs on the public, we must know where the viewers stand in their relation to God. On one end of the spectrum, I would estimate that about ten to fifteen percent of the public are firmly rooted believers in God and the Bible. These will never accept any explanation other than the biblical account. On the other end I would estimate there are about five to ten percent who are atheists or God haters, who are just as deeply rooted in their unbelief and hate, who will always opt for the alternative explanation. In between these two groups is what I choose to call the impressionable ones. They range from partial believers to almost atheists. These media offerings target that group which represents approximately 80-85 percent of the population.

Picture a member of this group who goes to church regularly, has heard the biblical message of salvation, he or she is under conviction of the Holy Ghost, and is almost ready to accept Christ. They turn on their TV and they see a program that says that Jesus was really married to Mary Magdalene and they had a daughter. The doubt and confusion this generates in their mind causes them to abandon their decision.

Picture the doubting Thomas that goes to church, but just can't bring himself to believe the gospel message without some kind of proof. He or she sees the same program and accepts this as proof that the biblical account is a farce, and never goes to church again.

Of course these are hypothetical, but let me tell you about an experience that happened to me recently. My wife loves to do paint by numbers pictures, and she has become quite good at it. If there ever was a paint by numbers picture with Christ in it on the market, she has painted it, and hung it in our living room. A young man who was in my home one day looked up at the DaVinci last supper and asked: "Which one of these is supposed to be a woman?"

This young man had fallen prey to the media hype. We immediately had a long talk!

There is a documentary that suggests that Mary Magdalene, as the alleged widow of Jesus, (a preposterous falsehood), was the real power behind the early church after his death on the cross. If this were even remotely true, then why is her name not mentioned in any of the historical writings about the early church? Mathew, Mark, Luke, John, Paul, Peter, Jude, Josephus, not a one mentioned her name. Yet, this is suggested as a distinct possibility. The proponents of this suggestion maintain that because the early church was totally male dominated, her contribution was purposely ignored. If the church was male dominated as they point out, then how could she become the power behind it? By suggesting a strong male domination, they are defeating their own argument. They also contend that the church kept the record of the marriage between Jesus and Mary Magdalene hidden so that they could falsely proclaim Christ's purity and chastity. Jesus was never married to anyone, nor did he ever have even one impure thought of any kind. Every single moment of his life was totally focused and dedicated to accomplishing the will of his Father. If this were not the case, then he could not have been God's sacrificial lamb, without blemish or spot, the savior of mankind; Christianity becomes a hoax, and we are all doomed to eternity in the lake of fire.

I have seen more than one program about secret codes being hidden in the text of the Bible, the DaVinci code being the most famous. Who put them there, and for what purpose? I hope that I have already convinced you that God controlled every aspect of the production and distribution of the Bible, and if so, what would be his purpose in allowing such a thing to happen? If these secret codes are in the Bible I use today, how about the original manuscripts? If they were in the original manuscripts they could not possibly be in the modern day Bible due to the vast difference in the two alphabets. I am not sure, but I believe that most of the bibles in DaVinci's day were written in Latin, a language that came in between the original languages of the scripture, and modern day English. After careful consideration I can only conclude that this suggestion that there are secret codes in the Bible is too far fetched a theory to merit our attention.

Another attempt to discredit the word of God by the media is to explain supernatural acts of God, such as the great flood, the parting of the waters, and the destruction of Sodom and Gomorrah by natural means. Numerous TV specials of late have been made attempting to explain these acts of God scientifically, discounting their divine nature. Modern man does not want to believe in the awesome supernatural power that was necessary for God to perform these acts, after all, the minions of science would have you believe that such powers could not exist in the universe. If mankind can explain these acts in some natural way then he does not have to believe that these powers exist. His alternate explanation of these acts negates even the suggestion of the existence of such power. This places God on a lower plane, renders him less threatening, renders the biblical explanations to be mere mythology, and eases man's dread of God's judgment. It even allows for doubt that the biblically described judgments will even happen.

I now want to focus on the printed media, namely the supermarket tabloids. Did you ever notice how they are always placed at the front of the store, usually right at the check out line? You can't help but notice their bizarre headlines as you wait to be checked out.

There is one in particular that specializes in religious news; I call it satan's funnies. This tabloid prints predictions from Mother Theresa, Nostra Damus, Edgar Caysee, and some so called Indian chief, to name a few. Their "facts" are confirmed by so called religious experts that I, for one, have never heard of, and they have predicted the end of the world at least twice a year for as long as I can remember seeing the headlines in the check-out line. The amazing thing to me is that people actually believe some of that tripe. (They must believe some of it, or they wouldn't waste their money on the magazines). The bizarre features contained in this magazine make a mockery of traditional Christian beliefs, and contribute significantly to the secular attitude that the practice of Christianity is fanatical, foolish, and that its precepts are false.

I cannot leave the subject of the printed media, without visiting the "Harry Potter" phenomenon. Not only did the book and movie series deal heavily with the mystic powers of the occult, but it tries to bestow an undeserved aura of respectability to witchcraft. The books received rave revues in a large segment of our educational system, and in some schools they became required reading. (California, where else!) I wish the Bible could get that much attention. As I pondered that thought, I came to an epiphany.

Using the same standards by which these people judged the Harry Potter series, there is little difference between it and the Bible. Before you call me a blasphemer, let me explain. Before anyone could find any positive value in the Potter books, they would have to be a non-believer. Even a moderate Christian would have to reject the series as vile and ungodly. Therefore, looking at the Bible from a non-believers standpoint, one could readily see all the secular attributes that drew them to Harry Potter. There is a similar portrayal of mystical and supernatural occurrences in the Bible, so why isn't the Bible required reading and enjoying the same wide acceptance? I can only assume that secular man is anti-God.

To put it all in perspective, the media is in the business of making money; if the truth of God is not popular then they just invent another "truth". Sensationalism sells!

By the way, Elvis is still alive and working at Wal-Mart!

CHAPTER FIVE

THE GOD OF THE MOVIES

When I was just a lad, it was a regular Saturday night ritual that our whole family would go to the movies. At risk of dating myself as quasi-ancient, this was before television; most radios were powered by batteries, and the stations signed off the air around 10:00 PM; and we had a crank type telephone on the wall that was connected to a party line. For a little less than a dollar, I could see a movie, as well as make an ample purchase at the refreshment counter.

Friday and Saturday nights were always western nights. I recall watching Gene Autry, Roy Rogers, Tom Mix, Hopalong Cassidy, Randolph Scott, Red Ryder, and of course an up and coming young cowboy star named John Wayne, as well as a host of others too numerous to mention. These men were my heroes. I would get a soft pine board and a jackknife, carve out a genuine colt 45 six-shooter, and chase imaginary bad guys all over our farm, emulating these men.

One thing about those old movies, you could be certain who the good guys and the bad guys were, and the good guys always won. Good moral values were always accentuated. Another thing about those heroes, they led the same exemplary life off the set because they realized that they were adored by young lads like me and they took that responsibility seriously. What a difference between them and the stars of today. The current crop is in and out of strange beds, in and out of marriage, in and out of rehab, and in and out of jail.

The movies that come out of Hollywood today must make the devil proud. They are for the most part, purely un-adulterated pollution for the soul. When the current trend first began, the excuse for the cursing, sex, and violence was that they were portraying realism. Now I don't know about you, but I get more than enough realism in my day to day living. For a respite, I would like to be entertained by some fantasy once in a while! Not the morbid fantasy that the movies of today offer, with blood, guts, flames, and gore, served up by hideous monsters of the nether world, and that give children life threatening nightmares, but the wholesome fantasy that is present in the old Disney films. Films that I can set and watch with my grandchildren like Peter Pan, Bambi, Jungle Book, and the Herbie series, to name a few. These movies were squeaky clean, and an uplifting experience. They had a positive influence on the psyche, and made one feel that life was really worth living after all.

In contrast, the fantasy offerings of today have the opposite effect. They appeal to the squalid nature of man, a nature that is best kept under extreme subjection. These movies have the same effect on the audience as the extravaganzas that were once held in the old Roman Coliseum, where gladiators were made to slay one another, and Christians were fed to the lions. The first time it is somewhat shocking and distasteful, but after repeated exposure, the "shock and awe" wears off and the emotional effect is diminished to the point that some of these spectators can commit heinous acts themselves with little or no remorse.

I recall when the movie Robo-cop came out. It was one of the first to incorporate filthy language in almost every line. The story line was about a policeman whose body had been mangled and he was rebuilt with body parts made from metal. He had the strength of ten men, and he was impervious to gunfire. My children wanted to go see it. When I commented about the filthy language, my oldest son tried to defend the movie with the remark: "But Dad that is realism. That is what life is really like." To which I replied: "And I suppose a one hundred horsepower cop made out of tin is realism too, right? You can't have it both ways, and you're not going to the movie." This was about twenty five years ago, give or take a few, but the movie Robo-Cop pales compared to what is on the silver screen today. These movies rarely teach any moral values, and if they do it is the new morality of: "If it feels good, do it", which is more an absence of morality than a behavioral code.

Just as I used to emulate those western heroes of my youth, our youth of today try to emulate what they see on the silver screen. A feeble attempt by secular mankind has been made to shelter them somewhat from the worst of these Hollywood offerings by establishing a rating system, but it is a farce. In my estimation, PG should stand for "pure garbage", and R should stand for "run for your life"! This rating system is seldom enforced, and is often used in reverse: "Oh goody! The movie we're going to see is R rated."

The computer world has a saying: "trash in, trash out". The human brain contains a monstrous data base of unfathomable capacity. I don't believe man has ever discovered its limits. First we saturate that data base with the kind of data that is provided in these films, and then we come to a point in life where we have to make a decision. The process that we most often use in making these decisions is to look back into that data base for past experiences and observations that correlate with the situation at hand. If there is no precedent in that data base for good behavior, then guess what? Our decision will be based on bad behavior, trash in, trash out! You may use the age old excuse, "that stuff doesn't affect me"; well, I'm here to tell you, if you have a typical human brain, it does!

The saturation of these films with smut has a deadening effect on the psyche. After repeated viewings of the trash, what was sensational the first time, becomes commonplace. Man's senses become deadened to the impact, and so he desires a deeper experience. The movie industry then ratchets up the smut content in the films, and the cycle repeats itself. Man soon becomes tolerant of this ungodly behavior, and after repeated exposure he accepts it as the norm. Taken to the extreme, he begins to believe that following God is bad for him, while following the devil is good. While God has not been changed by the process, man's perception of God has done a complete reversal.

Two particular movies that incensed the Christian world were "The Last Temptation of Christ", and "The DaVinci Code". Both of these movies were a direct affront to God and his biblical teachings.

34

This was not accidental. The industry would not have made these films if they didn't believe they would receive wide acceptance by the public. I believe their purpose was two-fold; first, to cast an enormous blight on God, His son Jesus, the founders of Christianity, and the Bible, and secondly of course, to make money.

The first movie is an attempt to humanize Christ and portray him as just like us, (heaven forbid). And the second attacks not only the Bible, but questions the honesty of those who produced it.

Going back to the impressionable ones that I mentioned earlier, there are many in that group who will gladly accept these offerings as truth, because in trusting in them they feel somewhat relieved in their responsibility to God, and therefore, they feel safer about their future.

In summary, the movie industry, following its own gods of fame, fortune and notoriety, feels comfortable attacking God, and trying to change man's perception of him. They also portray an alternate to the Christian lifestyle that is vile and ungodly, while never once examining its consequences.

An offshoot of the movie industry is the pornography market. The sale of porn videos, literature, and internet offerings is a multi billion dollar industry today. This industry is absolutely amoral and motivated solely by greed and lasciviousness. It caters to the most vulgar instincts of mankind. Minors are often exploited, and at times are held against their will and brutalized, all for profit.

Porn is just as addictive as tobacco, alcohol, or illegal drugs. While its proponents might argue that there is no physical component to porn addiction as in the other three, I submit that the psychological component is so strong as to more than make up for the lack. As a minister I have seen first hand the tragic destruction of spiritual, physical, and even financial family integrity that can be caused by porn addiction. As in all other vulgar pursuits, continued participation results in a desire for a more heightened experience, and often results in the commission of heinous sexual crimes.

In short, it is unwholesome, immoral, degrading to both the producer and the consumer, and more importantly, it is most ungodly.

While not an integral part of the movie industry, the two are closely related so we will discuss video games in this section. Probably the most popular game at the time of this writing is entitled: "Grand Theft Auto". The name should speak for itself. There are already four versions of it, and each version is a little more vile and offensive than the one before. This game is pure garbage, with no redeeming qualities whatsoever. The player takes on the character of a felon, and goes through life situations, committing as much crime as possible without getting caught. As you would imagine, filthy language and sexual activity are an integral part of the game. Sounds like a great pastime for the formative years of your children, huh? To be sure, you have to be eighteen or older to buy the thing, and most video stores will probably enforce that, but once the game gets home, how many parents will take positive steps to ensure that it does not ever get into the hands of their children? Some ultra-permissive parents actually buy the thing for their offspring, shame, shame!

This game is not unique, but it is rather typical of what the video stores have to offer. These games are full of violence, gruesome looking monsters, and some games graphically depict decapitations, and dismemberments as well as unimaginable torture of all kinds. The entire industry is completely amoral! I would submit that the average video game has become satan's WMD!

CHAPTER SIX

GOD IN SCHOOL?

A lady in our church wears a T-shirt that has this message written on the back:

> Dear God,
> Why is there so much violence in our public schools?
> Concerned student

> Dear concerned student,
> Sorry, I am not allowed in public schools.
> God

While this may be somewhat of an exaggeration, It is not far from the truth. Under the guise of "separation of church and state", a concept that was conjured up by gross misinterpretation of our constitution, active participation in organized daily prayer or worship has been banned and in some cases criminalized in our public schools. Whenever any Christian educator tries to re-establish any semblance of recognition of God in the classroom, the watchdog groups are immediately on the scene, demanding severe retribution. Even if the majority of parents and teachers wanted to re-install God in their local school, they would be prohibited from doing so under penalty of law.

What the constitution actually says is: "Congress shall make no law respecting the establishment of religion or prohibiting the free exercise thereof." Isn't telling a Christian student he cannot pray, he cannot mention God, or have any Christian materials on school property, "prohibiting the free exercise thereof"? You frequently hear that part of the constitution referred to as the "freedom of religion clause". How can it be called freedom if one is chastised for even the mention of God's name or having in their possession, printed matter of a religious nature, including the Bible? I find it somewhat strange that only the Christian religion is singled out. It sure seems to this old country boy that there is a skunk in the woodpile!

The ACLU which has appointed itself as the watchdog for any inappropriate conduct i.e. use of school facilities for religious activity, prayer at school graduations, sports events etc., instigated a lawsuit in the state of Virginia to allow a Wiccan "priestess" to open a town meeting with a humanistic prayer. Is that a double standard or what? I wonder who she prayed to.

There seems to be an effort of late to teach about, and to recognize Islam in our schools. I have heard of one case where all the students in a class, most of which had no connection with the religion of Islam, had been required, as a project, to take a Muslim name, and write an essay on what they would do for Allah. Can you imagine the uproar if they were required to take a biblical name and write an essay on what they would do for Jesus?

I also find it somewhat ironic that the very day that our Supreme Court judges made the decision to remove prayer from our public schools, they started their day with a prayer, as they always do. While they consider the school system to be part of government, do they consider themselves not to be? The Supreme Court has its own chaplain, the House of Representatives has its own chaplain, the Senate has its own chaplain, do they not have more to do with our governance than the school system does?

You may think this strange, coming from a minister of the gospel. But I partially agree with their original decision. While I consider it morally appropriate and personally desirable to open every school day with a spoken prayer, I must agree that it would be legally wrong in accordance with their interpretation of the constitution to mandate a specifically Christian prayer at the start of the school day. To a degree, this would constitute establishment of a state religion, and therefore be unconstitutional, but only if you include the school system as an integral part of the federal government. In my estimation it is not and therefore not subject to the principal of separation of church and state. The school is no more a part of our "body" of government than is the postal system. Neither the school, nor the postal system has any responsibility for administration, legislation, or adjudication of the law of the land. Apparently the Court did not see it that way.

When the constitution was written there was a local school system, answerable only to the community it served. In many cases, especially in small rural communities which were just starting up, the local church served as the school house during the week, or the school house served as the church on Sunday, depending on which was built first.

When our forefathers wrote the constitution I am reasonably sure that they did not have any desire that the federal government be involved in the day to day administration of our school system. The Federal government had no interest or responsibility, nor was any given in the constitution. The federal government has usurped power and authority that legally belong exclusively to state and local governments, not only in the area of school administration, but in many other areas as well. It is the desire of a majority of parents and a growing number of educators that control of the system be returned to local authorities, but once the monster gets its talons into the prey, it refuses to let go.

If open prayer cannot be allowed, I believe that the spoken prayer should have been replaced with a moment of silence to allow each person present to reflect on their own preference. Restricting any religion is expressly prohibited by the freedom of religion clause. Using their own logic, if it is unconstitutional for the school system to promote a particular religion, it is constitutionally required that they tolerate all forms of it uniformly!

This decision to eliminate prayer opened up a "Pandora's Box", and allowed radical, ungodly, institutions to use the decision as a lever to attempt the eradication of God from the minds of educators and students alike.

There seems to be a concerted effort today by groups such as the NEA and the ACLU to modify the curriculum from pure education to education plus indoctrination, heavy on the indoctrination. As a taxpayer, I would remind them that we pay them to educate only.

If I paid a man to fix the roof of my house, and I find him replacing a window, I am going to be upset. Get the picture?

The formation of a child's moral attitudes and lifestyle has long been the exclusive responsibility of the child's parents. You may disagree with me, but I find that obligation to be assigned by God in his Holy Word. One need only read the book of Proverbs, to see that God has given specific instructions on rearing and disciplining children. For the school system to interfere with this responsibility is for it to usurp authority it does not have, and more importantly, causes confusion in the minds of our children as to which set of values to adhere to. It does not take long for a child to realize that the school system is anti-God, perhaps not always by choice, but for sure by judicial decree. For families who are not believers in God, this does not create a serious problem, but for practicing Christian families, their children are often faced with two directly opposite opinions. Children who openly confess Christian beliefs in their scholastic associations are often treated as pariahs.

It seems to me that one of the criteria for a new concept or idea to be included in the curriculum these days is that it must be anti Christian. Text books, especially in the area of the social sciences, have become decidedly amoral. Instead of portraying the choices we encounter in life as "this is considered morally right and this is considered morally wrong", they teach: these are your choices, take your pick.

For an educator to teach the child of Christian parents that there is nothing morally wrong with a gay lifestyle is in direct contradiction to what those parents and their churches teach. The immoral nature of the gay lifestyle is clearly defined in the Bible, and no fundamental Christian could ever accept it as anything else, although our school system consistently tries to shove it down our throats as normal and wholesome. If a teacher wants to condone the homosexual lifestyle, that is their prerogative, but there is NO EDUCATIONAL BENEFIT to their actively propagating that belief.

There seems to be a concerted, sometimes covert effort to bring the homosexual lifestyle constantly before our children.

A case in point is Mr. David Parker, who lives in Lexington Massachusetts. Mr. Parker's child brought a book home from school that extolled the virtues of gay parenting. Incensed, he went to the school and reminded them that under Massachusetts state law, parents must be notified prior to such material being presented to students. When the school authorities did not seem to satisfy his complaint, he told them he was not leaving until he had a confirmation that the law would be honored. He was arrested, physically removed from the school to jail, and issued a restraining order. Under this order, he was not allowed on school property for any reason, thus being excluded from his children's activities such as band concerts, sports activities, and even graduations. I find it tragically ironic that this should happen in Lexington Mass., a city that was so significant in the birth of our national freedoms.

The school administrators have been brainwashed, cajoled and threatened into such actions by special interest groups who do not represent the mainstream thinking of most of today's parents. In order to promote their politically correct agenda, they must reinvent or banish God.

Now let us move on to our institutions of higher learning. I believe that one of the greatest detriments to a viable college education today is the concept of tenure. Once a professor achieves it, he becomes a little god in the class-room, and he is practically assured a job for life. He can propagate ungodly, radical, inflammatory, unpopular, even traitorous ideas, with absolutely no fear of dismissal, or retribution. A majority of these become narcissistic due to their established position and act like they have cornered the market on intelligence in their chosen field. Remember that many of these were among the protesters of the sixties. Many are more interested in promoting their own radical agendas than in preparing their students for life's challenges. To disagree with one openly will usually result in a public harangue, usually accompanied by a corresponding reduction in class grade, so many students are forced to endure a philosophy, or a principle that they do not espouse in order to receive a passing grade. Some of these succumb to the pressure and are converted to the professor's way of thinking.

The majority of college professors are liberal and atheistic in their thinking, or if they do believe in God, they have a very radical definition of him that usually contradicts the biblical description.

Using their position of authority, they are intent on turning all their students into carbon copies of themselves.

I have heard several conservative Christian scholars on television and radio complain about the unjust prejudicial treatment they receive whenever they try to exercise "free expression", (to use one of the mantras of academia). It seems that expression is only free so long as it agrees with the radical thinking of the academia elite.

Even many so called Christian schools have been infected with the blight. If a Christian school receives any federal money, or accepts any students that are receiving any kind of federal scholarship, there are severe restrictions placed on them regarding their employment policies, and the content of their curriculum. To be fair, there are still some Christian schools that doggedly cling to moral values but they do so at great cost. They choose not to receive federal monies as they would then be required to follow the federal guidelines for the use of these monies. This places them at a monetary disadvantage over the secular schools.

I do not place all the blame on the school system. I have spoken to educators who believe that teaching and maintaining biblical moral standards in the classroom would be extremely advantageous to the learning process. Some of them have on occasion bent the rules and tried to do this to some degree. I know parents who have lauded the bravery of these educators. Sadly their efforts are too little, too late, and when discovered, result in strict censure, or sometimes even loss of employment.

I feel very fortunate and blessed that in the school system where my grandchildren attend, there are a number of teachers who are openly Christian, and so far, to my knowledge, none of them have been persecuted in any way. I recall recently sitting in the gallery at a school board meeting that was opened in prayer, which I am told is their usual procedure. (I hope the ACLU doesn't read this as they would probably try to put a stop to the opening prayer).

Our school campuses have become playgrounds for satan and his henchmen. From pre-K to masters, most school curriculums either deny the existence of God or redefine him as suits their purpose. They discourage, and even on occasion punish any open recognition of his sovereignty over the human soul. By removing God from the classroom, we have created the atmosphere and conditions that culminate in disasters like the Columbine tragedy. We have removed God from the classroom, and replaced him with policemen in the halls!

CHAPTER SEVEN

THE MORAL BANKRUPTCY OF UNCLE SAM

Proverbs 30:
11. There is a generation that curseth their father, and doth not bless their mother.
12. There is a generation that are pure in their own eyes, and yet is not washed from their filthiness.
13. There is a generation, oh how lofty are their eyes! And their eyelids are lifted up.
14. There is a generation, whose teeth are as swords, and their jaw teeth as knives, to devour the poor from the earth, and the needy from among men.

Perhaps it is the onset of senility, but when I compare the lifestyle of today with the lifestyle of my youth, I see a marked increase in acceptable immorality. Respect for the elderly, and respect for the female of the specie is no longer practiced, and on most any main street in the USA one can hear God's name taken in vain, and vulgar language being shouted out as a matter of course, in mixed company. It seems to me that we are smack dab in the middle of the generation that is talked about in the above verses. (More Texas lingo). It is no wonder that secular mankind is fighting against exposure to the Ten Commandments as his conscience can't accept them anymore. National figures, athletes, politicians, judges, and religious leaders are instructed in God's word to be good examples to the public, and a majority of them in the past, complied with his instructions. Ever since the social revolution of the sixties, there has been a constantly increasing falling away from that practice. Instead of setting a good example, many have boldly defied God's instructions by setting a bad example, and then flaunting it.

A democracy such as ours, due to it's inherent freedoms, cannot endure without subscribing to time tested sound principals of moral and ethical conduct. The answer to all our social and economic ills of today cannot be found in the oval office, or the halls of congress, but in the pulpits and pews across our nation. Until our people, and especially our leaders, rediscover and practice Godly living, no amount of government intervention, no court edicts, or bills of law will make any difference. Morality cannot be legislated, it must be learned. In enjoying the freedoms of a democratic society, we also possess the tools of our own destruction.

The term "politically correct", coined during the waning years of the twentieth century, has become a religion of sorts, or at least a substitute for religion. More and more, the concept is treated reverently and considered to be the only acceptable behavior for modern man. In many cases, it has replaced rational thought. It has no absolutes as far as right and wrong, and it condones immoral and illegal behavior if the particular circumstances warrant such behavior in the mind of modern man. Political correctness subscribes to "situation ethics". For instance, thou shalt not steal does not apply if you are out of a job and your children are hungry. The situation dictates the degree of ethical conduct required. There are no moral absolutes in political correctness. A criminal is not a criminal by choice, but he is a poor, misunderstood, victim of society who just never was given a chance. Have I got news for him; chances are not given, they have to be earned! It was bad enough in the past when people made up excuses for themselves, but now we have the government and the courts making up excuses for them too. If political correctness is not a state substitute for religion, it sure comes mighty close!

The "inalienable rights" endowed on us by our creator as defined in the Declaration of Independence have been replaced by modern man with "civil rights" which are flexible and can be redefined at will, depending on the situation. The word inalienable and the benefactor, God have been taken out of the equation, making these rights cease to be inalienable. Suddenly man becomes the benefactor, and these rights are defined and administered by him. Whatsoever man giveth, man taketh away!

A case in point is the current misuse of the right of eminent domain. Since its inclusion in our constitution, it has been narrowly defined to mean that the government can force a property owner to give up his or her property, at a fair market valued price, but ONLY to facilitate a government enterprise, e.g. building a highway, a railroad, or developing a water reservoir etc. Recently our Supreme Court decided to widen the definition to include private enterprise as well. Here's how it works. The Ajax development corporation decides that your property would be a good location for a convenience store, so they approach you with the idea, and you decline their offer. All they have to do next is go to the city and show proof that the store would produce more tax revenue than you are currently paying. The court ruled that this increase in revenue for the city would benefit all of its residents, and therefore the rule of eminent domain would apply. In other words, you can keep your property only as long as Wal-Mart or 7-11 doesn't want it! I know of one small family owned business and even one church that this has happened to in Florida. These two entities, both of which had been established for a number of years at the same location, were in the zone of a proposed mega-mall. The last news I heard, both cases were in litigation, but the damage had already been done. There is no telling how many other property owners have fallen prey to this practice. Of course they have to pay you a fair market value, but is that fair and just? Let's use myself and my wife as an example. We live in a very old wood frame house appraised on the tax rolls at forty eight thousand dollars. How could we possibly replace it at today's market prices? What value can be placed on the memories of raising eight children there; on the anticipation of spending our "golden years" amongst familiar surroundings? This is not just our house, it is our home. Every time I look at it I reflect fondly on how we worked to pay it off and fix it up. If it were taken away to make way for a new highway, I would still feel the loss, but I would understand as that would seem reasonably in tune with the intent of the authors of our constitution, but if it were replaced by a convenience store I could see no justification at all. I would consider that to be an infringement on my God given inalienable rights. The fact that man has usurped the right of God to decide what is right and what is wrong makes it all legal.

How did our government get so inconsiderate of the common people? Most of our political leaders have an elitist attitude. Only they are smart enough to know what is good enough for you and me. They are even smarter than God so they are taking his place. Are they in for a surprise! I want God back!

"Washington is broken" was a popular mantra during the 2008 elections. Those politicians sure are slow. Most of us figured that out at least ten years ago.

Washington lobbyists and political action committees, (PAC), spend billions of dollars annually in questionable political contributions, "junkits", midnight soirees, and outright bribes. It doesn't take a rocket scientist to figure out that nobody in their right mind spends that kind of money without getting a return on their investment!

Let me explain how most of our laws come into existence. It usually starts with a PAC. They see a need for a particular law that will be favorable to the particular interest that they represent and they look for a legislator who either owes them a favor, or has shown some sympathy for their cause in the past. A "back room deal" is struck and the PAC volunteers to draft the bill. In this way, they can ensure that the language of the bill is totally favorable to their agenda. A little known fact is that legislators seldom write their own bills. The draft bills are sometimes written by congressional staffers, but more often directly by the PAC.

Another little known fact is that these bills, sometimes hundreds of pages long, are not always read by the legislators who vote on them, even the ones submitting the bill!

A prime example of this is the stimulus bill that was bulldozed through congress in the opening days of the Obama administration. This bill was hastily conjured up in answer to a highly inflated sense of urgency, was voted on and passed even before the congress which voted on it was fully aware of it's content, and it's inadequacy has yet to be fully realized. The stock market fell to less than half of it's peak of the previous year, and one financial expert called it the "largest destruction of wealth in the history of our nation."

The task of reading and analyzing these bills is often relegated to a paid staffer, who is not elected by the public, nor accountable to them. This staffer will then brief the legislator on the bill, but due to time constraints, this briefing is only a brief synopsis which will only be as accurate and un-biased as the staffer wants it to be. For a legislator to read all the materiel that they are required to vote on is physically impossible due to its sheer volume. This staffer doing the briefing was probably hired not so much for his credentials, as for his political assistance during the legislator's campaign for office.

Due to the ambiguity and complexity of this system, there are ample opportunities during the process for graft and corruption to enter in. It is my belief that the system has even been fine tuned by its users to facilitate such actions. Expecting congress to clean it up is tantamount to expecting the fox to return the chickens to the henhouse!

These politicians are seldom, if ever, caught by their peers, and if they are caught at all, it is usually by an outside investigative source. In the past, the news media pretty much held the politicians feet to the fire, but of late, whenever it serves their liberal agenda, they look at graft and corruption with a silent smile. Cronyism is practiced to the nth degree and political maneuvering has reached a height of shamefulness that is ungodly. When one of them is caught, instead of the peers demanding punishment, they circle the wagons, protecting the accused at any cost. I am reminded of an old adage: Birds of a feather flock together!

The political battles of the present have almost reached the status of a civil war. Instead of the North against the South, it is the Republicans against the Democrats. Instead of cannon and muskets, the weapons are lies, accusations, partisan politics, to include voter fraud, filibusters, gridlock and selective leaks to the press. While the battle rages, our infra-structure, our economy, and our reputation as a nation suffers. If we do not return to Godly ethics in our government, our nation will wind up on the trash heap with all the ungodly nations that have gone before. Effective governance has taken a backseat to search and destroy. Remember that famous line from the comic strip "Pogo", "we have found the enemy, and the enemy is us." The god of unrestrained power has reared its ugly head!

I would like to focus now on our judicial system. Our system of jurisprudence was God centered at its inception and based on *his* description of right and wrong. In diminishing the effect of godly principles in its process and administration, we have rendered the system less effective. The system that was based on the Judeo Christian ethic, which is summarized by the Ten Commandments, now bans the display of these very commandments in the courthouse!

Federal judges are appointed for a life term, and though there is a process for impeachment, I cannot recall that it has ever happened. This lifetime appointment system was designed to remove political pressures from influencing their decisions, and if the selection process was carried out in the proper manner, we would have highly qualified, unbiased judges, with no political agenda.

The problem we have today is that the selection process has become highly politicized. Candidates are selected more for their political philosophy than their expertise in jurisprudence.

Whenever one party controls the White House, and the other party controls Congress, the battle rages with petty bickering on both sides, and the end result is that we wind up with a shortage of judges in a system that is already strained to the limits. Quite often lesser qualified candidates are appointed simply because they will be acceptable to the other side. When one party controls both the White House and the Congress, appointees are selected who have the same political philosophy as the party in power. The tendency then is to select more radical appointees over moderates. In either case, the end result is courts that are extreme rather than mainstream, or are short handed. I believe that it is in the best interests of the nation for the president to appoint candidates that are neither radical right, nor radical left, but are centrists. This has rarely been done. Whenever the president appoints candidates that strongly hold his political views, the other side digs in their heels, and the battle begins. It seems that both the executive and the legislative branches are attempting to draft the judicial branch into their own ranks by practicing partisan politics to the very limits.

They have even gone past reasonable limits on several occasions. I cite the examinations of judges Bork, and Thomas as examples. It all amounts to a struggle for power. The reason our forefathers set up three separate branches in our government was so that no individual branch would be capable of despotism due to the constraints that could be wielded by the other two. Whenever the court becomes extreme liberal, or extreme conservative, the system of checks and balances becomes imperiled.

The end result of this politicizing of the system is courts that legislate law by judicial fiat. Rather than interpret existing law in a uniform manner, the court is on a political see-saw, and the scales of justice are always tilted toward whichever political ideology has the most judicial clout at the time.

For the past one hundred years, the trend in our judicial system has been toward liberalism. When our system was first established, it leaned heavily on biblical standards of punishment and restitution; justice was uniform and predictable. Fairness and justice were the predominate goals of the system. As we began to eliminate godly principles from the system we came further and further from achieving those goals. Mankind began to insert his own definitions of fairness and justice, and these were predictably tainted by his own biases and preferences. As a result, the system began to deteriorate. Uniformity became the victim of personal whim.

While minimum sentences have been established at the federal level, no such mandate exists at most local and state levels, and judges are free to exercise unreasonable judgment if they so desire. This has been occurring more and more of late, and the unreasonable judgments seem to always favor the accused rather than the victim. Certain ungodly behavior has become nearly acceptable in some of our courts. These unjust decisions often center on sexual crimes that are prohibited in the Bible, but modern enlightened man would like to see these prohibitions repealed for his own personal pleasure. When organizations like NMBLA (national man-boy love association) and the Gay Liberation Front are given recognition and a voice in the public forum, our nation has lost its moral compass!

The process of plea bargaining has become a widely accepted practice in our judicial system of today. It is designed to eliminate the need for overworked prosecutors to prepare and present a case. All too often our court dockets are filled to overflowing with low to mid caliber crimes. In order to ease the burden, prosecutors and judges often accept a plea for far less punishment than the crime deserves in exchange for a guilty plea. It is my belief that this practice actually causes an increase in criminal activity, defeating its own purpose. Let me explain:

This process allows for violators to commit crimes that they might not otherwise commit. Realizing that the probability of negotiating a plea bargain exists, they feel that the commission of a crime may be worthwhile. This creates a core of professional repeat felons, who don't mind spending a few months in jail between crimes; in fact, I am told by more than one correctional officer that some of these repeaters actually look forward to jail as a vacation from the worldly responsibilities of making a living, especially during inclement weather seasons.

If every state would adopt the "three strikes and you're out" rule, where the third felony would automatically carry a life sentence, this would help immensely. (I myself would favor a two strikes rule). The only problem there is that these jurisdictions are already drastically short of prison and jail space, which is another reason why extreme leniency is being practiced.

Even when a judge hands down a sentence, the felon seldom does more than two thirds of the time, and in many cases he does even less than two thirds. In my home state of Texas, the "twofer" rule applies in many cases. For every day that a felon serves without causing any trouble for the system, two days are taken off of their sentence. As an example, a crime that merits a ten year sentence could be plea bargained down to two years, and under the twofer rule the felon could expect to serve only one year, but due to the crowded conditions of the system, he stands a good chance of being paroled after six months. Pretty good deal, huh? Did I mention that while incarcerated the felon receives full medical, dental, and vision benefits at the taxpayers' expense?

If I was not aware of God's impending judgment, I would reject the old adage that "crime doesn't pay". Apparently many in our society have rejected it already!

Now let's talk about the "gimme" crowd. Out of the great depression of the thirties, "big brother" was born. The politicians discovered that desperate people were more than willing to surrender a portion of their liberty for a welfare check. Up until that time, the federal government had concentrated mainly on national issues and left the social issues to lower governments. As soon as federal monies began to be used for social programs, strict regulations were devised on how these monies were to be spent. Federal politicians soon learned that by catering to certain politically active groups, a faithful constituency could be assembled. By micro-management, and regulation of their assistance, they could manipulate these groups to a certain extent, and after continued association, these groups would become dependent on their benefactors. Quasi-socialism was born. The majority of those in power were not interested in elevating the standard of living for those on welfare; quite to the contrary, maintaining the status quo ensured them of a controllable constituency.

We are now in the third generation of this constituency, which has expanded in numbers to the point that the taxpayers can no longer shoulder the burden. When we request that the government cut back on some of these benefits we are branded as mean spirited, evil capitalists! The recipients of this welfare state have come to expect these benefits as a right that belongs to them, rather than the benevolence of a thoughtful neighbor.

I do not place the blame entirely on these hapless individuals; they have been duped, brought under subjection, and then exploited purely for political gain. Their exploitation is sinful, and is the result of the absence of godly moral principles of conduct in government. Jesus taught again and again that leaders should be servants and not masters. To subject any person to any form of involuntary servitude is contrary to what he taught, and in essence, this control of welfare recipients is a mild form of slavery!

It is far, far easier to fall into the mentality of welfare dependency than it is to get out. Such dependency usually results in a wasted lifetime of failure, non-productivity, and low self esteem.

Permit me to illustrate our present plight with a little story.

Many years ago fifty people decided to move about seven days journey from where they were.

The only transportation they had was one wagon, with no draught animals to pull it. Because of their numbers, they decided they could pull the wagon themselves.

On the first day, there were five people who, due to sickness, or other infirmities, could not contribute to the pulling, so the leader told them to ride in the wagon. Forty five were enough.

On the second day, five of the frailest among them were simply too exhausted to continue pulling, so they too were told to ride in the wagon; after all there were still forty.

On the third day, some of the forty began to complain. "Why should we have to strive in this hot sun all day, while the others get to ride in the wagon? It's simply not fair." Five of these faked exhaustion so that they too could ride in the wagon. Now there are only thirty five.

On the fourth day, five of the thirty five decided to slack off, and only pulled on the rope when the leader was looking. Soon, five more, noting that the original five were getting away with their slackness, joined in the malingering. The twenty five that were still pulling became exhausted at mid-day, and their journey ended, three days short of their goal. The wagon had become heavier, and the workers less in number.

Of course, this is just a story but it makes a very significant point. There are entirely too many people today riding the wagon, and entirely too few pulling the rope. It's as simple as that!

The attitude that some have a right to just drift along, depending on the productivity and benevolence of others is altogether too prevalent today. God expects us to be self sufficient, and earn our way to the best of our ability, depending on him when we need assistance, not on the substitute god of government.

God states in second Thessalonians, chapter three, and verse ten: *For even when we were with you, this we commanded you, that if any should not work, neither should he eat.*

Again in the same chapter, in verse twelve: *Now them that are such we command and exhort by our Lord Jesus Christ, that with quietness they work, and eat their own bread.*

Don't get the idea that I am against all forms of welfare. God gave the responsibility to care for the needy to the church, and the church has allowed the government to take it over.

There are some members of our society that truly need assistance, some temporarily and some permanently, and I fully support their receiving it, but I would venture to say that for every one of those, there are ten more who are milking the system and could adequately care for themselves if they had a desire to. If these ten were removed from the rolls, the rest of us could manage the wagon with ease, but the government doesn't seem to want that to happen.

We have become a society of whiners and complainers. One concept that arose during the sixties social revolution was the idea of equal distribution of wealth. "From each according to his abilities, to each according to his need." Sounds like a Godly concept huh? Actually it is a quote from Karl Marx in his communist manifesto!

Our federal government has become involved in so many facets of our lives that they are already task saturated. Their answer to the problem is to institute more programs, take on more responsibility, and use more and more of our money.

As an example, in the shadow of the social security debacle, they now want to take over our health insurance industry. If they cannot adequately handle the present workload, taking on more work is definitely not the answer!

Eighty percent of American households pay more in social security taxes than they do in income taxes, yet the system is in deep peril. In 1935, when the social security program began, there were twenty five workers to share the burden for each retiree. Due to growth in the number of recipients, this number was reduced in 2002 to 3.2, and it is estimated to go down to two workers per retiree in the year 2030. The latest estimates by the social security administration are that by the year 2015, outgoing payments will for the first time exceed receipts; by the year 2040, receipts will account for only seventy one percent of obligations. We are talking billions of dollars!

Congress has seen this coming for years, but no one has had the intestinal fortitude to address the issue. Both sides of the aisle conveniently blame partisanship for the inactivity. Any solution other than privatization would be extremely unpopular with the voting public. While privatization is the most popular solution among the electorate, congress has soundly rejected it. It seems they don't want to lose any portion of their power over the people.

Now they want to take over our health insurance industry. They use the excuse that millions of Americans cannot afford health insurance, and this is true, but those same people who cannot afford it still have access to health care if they have a genuine medical emergency regardless of their inability to pay for it.

One need only to look at the European nations that have had government controlled health care for several decades, to see that the only blanket coverage that the government (the taxpayer) can afford is substandard, inadequate, and costly. In some cases, people have actually died waiting for treatment to be scheduled! Canada has nationalized health care, and thousands of Canadians come across the border to purchase health care that cannot be adequately provided by their "free" system in a timely manner.

In summary, mankind has taken the liberty of replacing God as the director of our society in the arenas of politics and jurisprudence, and society as a whole has suffered for man's blunder. When moral values relax, the nation declines. We are following in the footsteps of corrupt nations long gone. Our government is afflicted with the cancer of ungodliness. By ignoring godly principles in its day to day administration, it has developed a case of terminal immorality. Only doctor God can administer the cure.

I echo the thoughts of Bob Hope when he said: "One sure way to make sure that crime doesn't pay is to legalize it and let the federal government operate it." (Sometimes it seems to me that we are well on the way to doing that!)

A wise man once said: "Man, by his very nature, is destined to strangle in his own physical and moral pollution".   It seems he was right!

CHAPTER EIGHT

WHERE ARE THE HEROES?

One thing that encouraged righteous living when I was a young man was the fact that I had heroes to look up to. Nearly all of them epitomized the virtues of honesty, goodness, and correct behavior.

Of course, my all time favorite hero on earth was dear old Dad! I was fortunate to have grown up on a dairy farm where my Dad, instead of bringing home the bacon, raised the bacon at home. That meant I got to spend a lot of time at his heels. As soon as I was old enough to navigate, I was expected to be one step behind him at all times. Just following in his footsteps had a major impact on the formation of my moral values that have stood me in good stead up until now. He was a strict but fair disciplinarian, who abhorred dishonesty in any form. While I will readily admit that my opinion is somewhat biased, I cannot recall even one moment that he ever did anything unjust or immoral in my presence. As busy as he was in trying to eke out a living on a farm that was too small to adequately support our family, whenever I asked a question, he always took time to satisfy my curiosity. Growing up during the great depression years, he only had three years of school, but his wisdom amazed me. What he lacked in formal education, he more than made up for in common sense.

Another thing he always took time out for was church on Sunday. If we had company early on Sunday morning as we often did, he or mom would tell them: "You can come to church with us, or else make yourselves at home; we'll be back when church is out."

Growing up in Sunday school, I learned of Bible heroes, and the Ten Commandments, and of course of Jesus, the Son of God. Next would be the cowboy movie heroes that I mentioned in a previous chapter, and close on their heels were sports figures. As WWII occurred during my formative years, (3 to 8 yrs old), there were also war heroes to look up to. I spent forty years in military and civil aviation, and the major influence in my career choice was hearing and reading about the exploits of the wartime aviation heroes of WW II. They played a major role in the development of the moral standards that I subscribe to today.

If I was a young man growing up today, I can't help but feel that my life would probably turn out quite differently. The influences that I have mentioned would be non-existent or at least greatly diminished.

They don't make dads like they used to. Due to the divorce rates of today, I dare say that more children have step-fathers than natural dads. One day while working in the church office, I was discussing with my wife, the tragic lack of commitment to marriage that is prevalent today. I came to the realization that I could not think of even one family in our congregation where Dad and all the children shared the same last name.

All too often when divorced people remarry, the children are considered just unwanted baggage that came with the deal, especially when only one parent has children. Under those circumstances it is hard for the child to find a hero there, or for the dad to be one. All too often the dad's attention is split between two households. His new family, and the one he left behind. Not only is that a problem, but he is often working two jobs, just so he can pay his child support.

While we are on the subject of divorce, I am sure most everyone will agree with me that a high divorce rate is detrimental to a society as a whole. It is especially traumatic on the children yet they have little or no representation in the proceedings, while, in most cases they are innocent victims of the process. I would like to see the individual states pass laws that if Mom and Dad want a divorce, then they would each have to share the financial burden of providing a legal advocate for the children also. While this is just a fantasy of mine, I would like to see laws passed that in cases of no-fault divorce, if the children did not agree that a divorce was necessary, the decree would not become final until the children became of age. They should not be made to suffer for their parent's lack of commitment.

Children of divorcees are much more likely to become juvenile delinquents, especially when they are suddenly faced with only a single parent. They more often than not deeply resent that parent's decision, and rebel forcefully against their authority. I am so thankful that I spent my entire childhood in a secure close knit family where the option of divorce was never even contemplated.

I can't speak for the girls, but I know that for a boy, the presence of a respectable Christian father is the most important influence in forming his character. I know it was in mine. I strongly suspect that the statement can also be made for girls and mothers.

Even if a child today has good Christian parents, their influence is offset to some degree by what these children see outside the family. I would estimate that children today spend only about half as much time at home under parental supervision than I did when I was growing up. They spend time in daycare, youth clubs, after school activities, and sleep-overs, therefore, it is essential that these outside influences be positive. This is not always happening today, and the children suffer for it. They turn to gangs, and rebellious behavior, because there is little positive influence in their lives.

I used to travel around the country a lot, and I always made a mental note of church signs. You know the kind with catchy little slogans or phrases on them. I remember one that read: "A child brought up in Sunday school is seldom brought up in court."

Sunday schools are not bound by the concept of political correctness, and they teach children the way God meant for them to be taught. There are two basic concepts taught there that are either severely watered down or nonexistent in the secular world. First, that right and wrong are absolutes. There is no such thing as almost wrong or almost right, and secondly that regardless of the circumstances we are ultimately responsible for our actions.

The secular world teaches us to make excuses. One facet of political correctness is the idea that no-one is ever one hundred percent guilty, that there are always mitigating circumstances. Even religion can be used as an excuse, (As long as it isn't Christianity). There were people in our own back yard who excused the diabolical murderers of 9/11 by blaming our intolerance of their religion for their heinous act. One preacher when preaching a sermon in the aftermath of 9/11 made the statement "America's chickens have come home to roost."

Aside from Christian homes, the only place in our society today where right and wrong are taught as absolutes, and responsibility is taught as a personal imperative is in Sunday school.

The next major influence we will discuss is the movie industry. In a previous chapter I pointed out the difference in behavior of movie stars between then and now, but why is there such a difference?

The movie industry of today is a product of the new liberal attitude toward morality. Most of the current seasoned actors and the financial and administrative powers of Hollywood came out of the sixties social revolution. Having fame and fortune thrust upon them, most did not possess the moral fiber to handle their new found freedom. Their thirst for freedom of expression could now be quenched and they zealously built a bastion of ungodliness. The younger stars of today are thrust into a caste system where they must either conform or step aside. I am not excusing their behavior; I am merely explaining the reason for the change. None of those folks were forced into that lifestyle. They each made a conscious choice to become part of what I consider to be a failed social experiment. They have "sown the wind, and now reap the whirlwind." (Hosea 8:7) By denying the authority of God and making up their own rules, they have created a leviathan that is consuming them.

There is such a strong liberal power base in the industry that if anyone "rocks the boat" they suddenly find themselves unemployed. Movie stars like Gregory Peck, John Wayne, Bob Hope, James Stewart, and William Holden to name a few, would have a hard job finding work today. There is a "street gang" mentality and loyalty to the "gang" has reached an almost religious fervor.

Let's look at Mel Gibson, and the movie "The Passion". While Mel Gibson is somewhat of a rebel by Hollywood's standards, fortunately, at the time he made the movie, he had achieved the tenure and notoriety that he could not be totally ignored. The fact that he financed the film with his own money leads me to believe one of two explanations. Either the financial moguls would not touch it because of its content, or Mel Gibson chose that route in order to secure complete independence from their influence. In either case, the powers to be loudly voiced their disapproval. There is no doubt that the making of the film has done harm to his career, but I don't think he has any regrets. Way to go Mel! We need more like you.

Now we come to sports figures. One of the main problems I see in today's sports stars is the fact that they are treated more as chattel than as personalities. They are bought and sold and traded much in the same way one would deal with race horses or greyhound dogs. Their futures are totally at the whim of a select group of millionaires. Their net worth is measured solely by their performance on the field of competition. The better performers are given a blank check where their conduct is concerned, as long as they can make touch-downs, home runs, goals, or baskets. These blank checks are not only granted by their owners, but by the fans, and even at times by the courts. Their escapades are for the most part, overlooked or treated as the harmless acts of high spirited young men. As long as these blank checks are written, there will be misconduct. Where is the call to high caliber sportsmanship and righteous living that permeated the original Greek Olympic games?

The competition has become so intense, and the moral component of sportsmanship so lax, that if an owner or a coach tried to revive these standards, they would lose their competitive edge. Can you imagine a coach today benching a key player solely for some misconduct on his part? The fans would be irate and the owner would probably fire the coach.

I heard a sportscaster on the radio tell the story of a particularly rowdy football team who put twenty two people on the field for their opening game. The referee demanded an explanation from the coach who said: "There are eleven players and eleven probation officers." Totally fictitious of course, but it makes a statement.

The Dallas Cowboys football team recently signed a multi-million dollar deal with a player who was incarcerated at the time of the signing. Upon release from his incarceration, his reputation for misconduct was such that the team actually assigned bodyguards to attempt to control his conduct when he was traveling with the team. He got in trouble anyway. What a hero!

To be fair, there are a lot of good wholesome players in sports today, but you seldom hear about them. You'll never hear a sports caster say: "Player X went through the whole season without so much as a parking ticket. He is active in his church and he prays before every game." What you will hear is: "Player Y was arrested today by the police for DUI, speeding, and resisting arrest. At the time of the incident he had a drunken prostitute in his Jaguar XKE."

To be truthful, there are more player X's than player Y's, but the up and coming young athletes only hear about the Y's. They also note that the Y's usually get little or no punishment. After all, what does a ten thousand dollar fine mean to a man making five million dollars a year?

An issue that has received a lot of notoriety of late is the use of performance enhancing drugs. The use of these drugs allows the user to break records that they would not have been able to do normally, a feat that is totally unfair to the previous record holder.

It is a universally recognized fact that these drugs have catastrophic effects on the human body. Shouldn't they carry the same penalty as the use of hard drugs such as heroin, opium or cocaine? While the athletes who use them receive some chastisement they seldom receive "hard time". The use of these drugs has become so widespread that some athletes reluctantly use them in order to remain competitive, although they strongly resent having to do so.

As long as such misconduct is tolerated, even adulated at times, there is little to look up to in the sports world as we see it.

I once heard a defense attorney for a misbehaving sports figure make the statement during a newscast: "after all, you can't expect them all to be choir boys." Yes, we can, yes we should, but sadly we don't!

Now let's look at war heroes. In WWI we had Sgt York, in WWII we had Audey Murphy, and in the Viet Nam war we had Lt Calley of Mhe-Lai. Why do I list them that way? I am just following the example of the media. These men were the most

62

talked about personalities in the media in each of these wars. While Lt. Calley was not considered a hero by any means, he was in fact probably the most famous and most discussed in the media of all our military personnel of that war. Whether or not he was guilty of anything other than the use of poor judgment was probably never proven, but he was tried and crucified over and over again in the liberal press of the day.

In WWI and WWII, the media was "on board." Their reporting was positive and upbeat, and more importantly, uplifting to the American public. The positive influence of the heroes of these wars was amplified by glowing media reports of their exploits, and this influence rallied a whole nation around the flag. Women put off their aprons and built airplanes, children with little red wagons circulated around the countryside collecting cans and anything recyclable for the war effort. I can remember my brother and I doing this with our red "Radio Flyer". In school, and at the post office, children purchased stamps to glue in a book that when filled, could be turned in for a victory bond. Young men signed up in droves, some even lying about their age, so they could possibly become heroes too. It was a glorious time and the media was right in there urging us forward.

Along came the Korean war and the media began to cool somewhat. They developed a kind of stand-offish attitude as though they had no stake in the outcome. Such objectivity is actually a desirable trait in peace time, but I feel that when a country is at war, the press has an obligation to be a rallying point for the populace. The press has the unique capability of influencing public opinion and recruitment like no other facet of our society. I am not suggesting that they should forego reporting the truth, but the truth can be told optimistically or pessimistically. (The war is nearly won; the war is nearly lost.) During the Korean War the reporting was neutral. (We are at war.) They did, however, mention the exploits of our war heroes favorably.

In Viet-Nam, the press turned completely around from their attitude of the previous three wars. They were decidedly anti-war, and their reporting shamelessly showed it. Instead of influencing young men to enlist, they were encouraged to burn their draft cards and flee to a foreign country.

Their reporting became so slanted at times that it was completely fictitious. As a case in point, I was stationed in Viet-Nam during the 1968 Tet offensive. The Viet Cong and the North Vietnamese threw everything they had at us, and we beat them back at every turn. They suffered thousands upon thousands of casualties, depleted nearly all of their stockpiles of war material, as we fought them to a standstill.

What did the folks back home hear? It was a stunning victory for the North! They almost overran the hamlet of Hue, they almost overran Saigon, they almost captured our embassy, and they almost captured the Marine base at Khe-San. Pardon me, but almost only counts in horseshoes. We didn't withdraw, they did. When the smoke had cleared away, the battle lines were the same as before, except they were breathing a heck of a lot harder then we were! We were still in possession of Hue; we were still in possession of Khe-San; we were still in possession of our embassy and the capitol of Saigon. Our mission was not to conquer, merely keep them at bay. Mission accomplished!

The media tried to make the public believe that the war was fruitless at that point, even lost. They cited our rising casualty rate as evidence that the war was turning against us, but made no mention that we had just stopped a major offensive, and therefore a rise in casualties should be expected. They concentrated on every mistake that was made but made little or no mention of the successes. Anyone who has been there will tell you that mistakes happen in combat. Because of the fluidity and rapid development of the situation, snap decisions have to be made, often with inadequate intelligence. A wise general once said, "A good battle plan always stays on track until the first shot is fired." Our counter offensive was conducted in a very professional manner, and our successes by far outnumbered the mistakes. More importantly, it stopped the enemy in his tracks and rendered him unable to continue the pressure, but it was not reported that way.

Their doom and gloom reporting achieved enough success that the public outcry became: "bring our boys home now." The victory that we achieved was negated by a few dishonest newsmen with a personal anti-war agenda. I had comrades who made the ultimate sacrifice in that campaign, and I found it extremely hard to forgive these press people for their disservice to the military, to their country, and to me personally.

Let's take a look at the war in Iraq. Can you give me just one name of a war hero from that war? Do you know how many Medal of Honor winners there have been so far? Unless you have a friend at the Pentagon, you will never know. The press will never report that information, but let a soldier, in the heat of battle, make a snap decision that MIGHT be questionable, and he is tried, convicted, and tarred and feathered on page one of the next days newspaper.

In short, whether or not we have war heroes, whether or not our cause is considered honorable by the folks back home, whether we come home to a heroes welcome or chants of "baby killer" depends largely on the news reports. I would like to end this segment with an open question to the news media of today. Do you think the late great Ernie Pyle would be proud of your reporting today? If you don't know who Ernie Pyle was, I rest my case! He was just the most highly regarded war correspondent this country has ever had. He lived in foxholes with his typewriter, ate "C" rations with the troops, and died a soldier's death on the front lines in WWII, during the battle for IwoJima from a Japanese sniper's bullet.

In short, the heroes of the past are just that! They have been replaced with liberal actors and actresses who thrive on lewd notoriety, dishonest politicians who will sell their soul for a bloc of votes, judges whose personal agenda overrides the constitution of these United States, sports figures who worship the mighty dollar, and even worse in our inner cities, by gang lords, pimps, and dope dealers. God help us!

CHAPTER NINE

THE FAMINE OF TRUTH & HONESTY

I believe that one of the gravest faults of our present society is the fact that hardly anyone can be trusted anymore. Honor has taken a back seat to greed and dishonesty. Remember the story about Abraham Lincoln for which he received the nickname "Honest Abe"? He allegedly walked several miles to a store because the storekeeper had given him two cents too much change, just to return the two cents. Such honesty is extremely rare today.

A popular mantra today is "what's in it for me?" This attitude is not only prevalent in secular society, but in the church as well. I would estimate that nearly half of the churchgoers of today attend not to serve God, but to be served by him! A number of these depart in disgust when their selfish desires are not met. They either stay at home, loudly criticizing the church and God, or they move from church to church taking advantage of each one's benevolence until they wear out their welcome, then move on to the next.

There are thousands of people today who make their living from the goodness of God's people. When I was pastor of a small country church, I had to deal with this frequently. I recall one instance when a family came to me with a gas bill for their home. They told me that their gas would be cut off if not paid the next day. I happened to notice that the date on the bill was four months old, and I turned them down. I later found out that this family went to nearly every church in the area, with similar requests, in order to get money to play bingo!

As another example, I received a phone message from a family who had children, and they said they had no food in their house. Our church had a small food closet, so one of the deacons and I took some food to their residence.   When we arrived, we noted that they lived in a very old house trailer, and we had to actually kick empty beer cans off of the steps in order to enter.   We left the food, for the children's sake, but I told them that this was the last time the church would assist them in their drinking habits.

One of the boldest incidents I knew of during my time as pastor concerned our church bus.   It wasn't actually a bus, but a maxi-van. Like a lot of churches, our bus was kind of old, and mostly powered by prayer.   Whenever we went out of town to a fellowship meeting or conference, we did a lot of praying until we got back home. (Sometimes I think God provides us with those old busses just to teach us how to pray).   To make a long story short, I found out later, that our driver had used that old dilapidated bus to take his family on an out of state trip of approximately two thousand miles without asking permission.

Just when I thought I had seen it all, a young man visited our church for the first time, and during the invitation, he came forward and requested to be baptized.   I told him he could be baptized on the next Sunday.   After the service, one of the people who came with him told me that he was a felon, and wanted the baptismal certificate in an assumed name in order to change his identity.   I checked on their story, and found it to be true.   Of course, I did not baptize him!

All of these people could not possibly believe in the same God that I believe in, or they wouldn't dare to try to con him and his people that way.   All of these families, with the exception of the baptismal candidate, were members of our church whose attendance was sporadic, with the exception of the bus driver, who for the most part attended regularly.   At some time in their past, they had made a confession of faith and been baptized.   I can only assume that their confessions were at least, partial fabrications, and they had the audacity to believe that they could pull a fast one on God!

I once heard a seminary professor on a television talk show state that he believed that God and the devil were not real, but were merely figure-heads for the opposing forces of good and evil.   And to think, this man is teaching young men and women to lead God's people.   What a travesty of God's trust!

I also heard a "feminist Christian" (her description, not mine), on another talk show, tell of her experience in attending a conference of women, where they gathered to "rethink" the male dominated scriptures. After careful consideration, and careful analysis, they discovered that God is really feminine, and her name is Sophia! And all this time I thought---; Oh well, back to the drawing board, I guess.

The reason I am citing these examples is to show that not everyone's definition of God is the same. Everyone seems to want to place God into their own niche. God is male, God is female, God is white, God is black, God is brown, God is yellow, and if you could speak the language of my miniature Doberman Pincer, she would probably tell you that God likes Alpo, and barks at passing cars.

God is uniquely God! He does not favor any portion of our society more than any other. I hear people claim "God made me in his image". I submit that that is absolutely not true, God made Adam and Eve in his image. I stand today, in the image of sinful Adam after the original sin. It shows in my countenance, in my attitude, in my psyche, and in my demeanor. I believe there was a definite change in mankind brought about by the original sin. Whether this change was wrought by God immediately at the time of Adam's fall, or occurred in a gradual deterioration caused by our sins, modern man falls far short of the image of God. Sin has a definite detrimental effect on the human body and psyche that is cumulative. Did you ever meet a drunk or dope addict that immediately reminded you of the image of God? Don't insult God by claiming that modern man is created in his image! I will one day be transformed into his image, but not in this life. My soul already belongs to Jesus, but I must deal with this sinful adamic body until he decides to take it away. Here is a radical thought; instead of changing our definition of God to be more like us, why don't we change our lifestyle to make us more like him?

With all this misinformation and misconduct going on in the Christian community, is it any wonder that many in the secular world are confused? When they look at us, can they see a clear manifestation of God's character and purpose?

I fear that what they see is much more confusing than enlightening. These people are, for the most part, skeptical to begin with. They can be watching a whole group of Christians and only one steps out of line; "I knew it, they're ALL a bunch of hypocrites!"

This places a tremendous burden on us to be on our best behavior, especially when out amongst the secular world. Most Christians, me included, seem to do just the opposite. We save our best behavior for church, and when out on the street, we sometimes let our hair down. Come on, you know you've done it.

While most of us do it only occasionally, there are some people who make it a practice. They are part time Christians. They feel that by spending two or three hours a week in church, they have satisfied their responsibility to God, and the rest of the week belongs to them. A case in point happened when I was working on a road team for a defense contractor. It was Friday evening, and I was on my way home for the week-end, with three other team members in my car. As was my custom, I had the radio tuned to a Christian station, and one of the passengers, who, I might add, was a deacon in his church asked me "Can you please change the station? I get enough of that on Sunday." What a witness for the other two passengers!

Some Christians become very nonchalant about their sins, because they know that God forgives. This is living on dangerous ground. It seems to me to be mighty close to taunting God. You may say "forgive me Lord for what I am about to do," and I have heard Christians use that phrase, but I can tell you with almost certainty that he is not going to do it. When you are finished, you are going to take a trip to the wood-shed! Don't ask me how I know that.

I have even heard some Christians say, "What I did must be OK because God let me do it." Using that logic, what Jack the ripper, Al Capone, and the Zodiac killer did was OK, right? Come on! That kite just doesn't fly. Just because God gives us the freedom to do something stupid, does not mean that he approves of the action.

One of the missions that God gave the church was to be a moral compass for society, A "Lighthouse on the hill", if you will. We are instructed to *let this mind be in you, which was in Christ Jesus.* (Phillipians 2:5)

I know everyone is familiar with the old adage: "A chain is only as strong as its weakest link". The moral standing of the church is only as pure as its weakest part. As long as the church tolerates immoral and sometimes illegal behavior, its light will grow increasingly dim.

I am not criticizing the church as a whole. The majority of churches and church members are striving to fulfill their obligations, but the secular world does not look at the church as a whole. It looks for the bizarre, and brands the whole with that identification. While it is politically incorrect to profile in any other area of society, that rule does not seem to apply when dealing with Christianity and the church. We are all hypocrites, we are all money grubbers, we are all do-gooders we are all teetotalers. These presumptions are false, and do not describe the majority of God's people, but that is how many in the secular world describe us.

That used to bother me tremendously until I came to the realization that I didn't have a problem, they did. There is no argument that will reverse an idea that is already formulated in a closed mind, so why try? I will try my best to convince them by my ACTIONS, and if that still doesn't work, oh well. I will continue trying to do God's work, and live God's way to the best of my ability, and pray for their immortal souls.

When I began this chapter, I did not intend to focus on the church, rather on the lack of honesty in the secular world, but any writer will tell you that sometimes an idea comes to mind, and will not let go until it is written down on paper. This was the case here. I kept asking myself, "What am I doing here?" and a little voice said WRITE! I seem to have satisfied that little voice, so now let's get on to my original thought.

It is becoming harder and harder to receive a fair deal today. Dishonesty along with its resultant distrust is rampant in every facet of our daily lives. The news of current events is almost always slanted to favor some hidden agenda, products seldom live up to their advertised performance, verbal promises are worthless from both a practical and a legal standpoint, and written contracts have become so complicated with legal loopholes and fine print that the average person is dumbfounded when trying to interpret them.

The dishonesty of our society today has spawned a multi billion dollar litigation industry that is unequaled anywhere on the planet. While the United States contains only a small portion of the world population, it employs nearly half the world's lawyers! Frivolous law suits are costing the American taxpayer billions annually, with no end in sight.

The distress caused by these conditions has caused most of society to become introvert to the extent that they create buffer zones between themselves and the rest of the world. This fortress mentality aggravates the distrust, and restricts us from having mutually advantageous relationships with those around us. Instead of interacting with our neighbors, we erect privacy fences!

This mentality also aids the devil in his quest to destroy God's people. The Bible says that he goes: *to and fro upon the earth, seeking whom he can devour.* It is much easier for him to devour one who is cowering in a darkened corner, than one who is surrounded by stalwart companions. Why does attending church regularly suddenly come to my mind?

This state of mind also greatly hinders Christians from performing the evangelical task that God has assigned them in Mathew, 28:19 *Go ye therefore, and teach all nations,---* We can't teach them if we cringe from the thought of associating with them.

When God designed man, he created in him a desire for companionship. Without this desire for companionship, man would have no reason to pursue a relationship with God. This was not selfish on God's part, because this relationship was to be mutually beneficial to both man and God. (More so to man than God) God also gave man a desire for companionship of his own kind. The self induced isolation brought about by the ills of the modern society we live in is contrary to that desire. The more isolated our fortress becomes, the greater the need to satisfy this desire grows. In order to satisfy that desire, we join groups of people who have the same interests. We join hobby groups, social clubs, fraternal groups, political organizations, and religious groups.

Right here I would like to insert a very salient point. The absolute best group to join is the family of God through the local church!

Many of the social and fraternal organizations include God in their rituals, but in order to appease every religion and belief, they depersonalize him, and veil him in obscurity to the extent that one size fits all. God to them is more of an "it" than a "he". He is described as a "higher power", or "supreme being", but they have only a vague understanding of his personality or purpose. Some church leaders as well as several people who call themselves Christians have followed their lead in the depersonalization of God.

On the dark side, some join street gangs and other criminal groups such as the skinheads, and the KKK. Both of these groups claim to believe in Christian principals. Their ultra-gross misinterpretation of these principals is about as far from Godliness as you can get.

Much has been said about the special camaraderie that exists between brothers in arms in combat. As one who has experienced this I can truthfully say that this bond is very close and extremely memorable. While not everyone can experience this feeling of kinship, the camaraderie of criminal activity by a street gang comes fairly close. While the goals of comrades in arms and comrades in crime are totally opposite, the bonding is much the same. I believe that is why such gangs are so popular today, and why the members are so dedicated to one another. These gangs are being popularized today in television documentaries, and there is no doubt in my mind that these documentaries aid these gangs in recruiting members. While their exploits are fairly well documented, the members are somewhat glamorized much the same as were Robin Hood and his merry men.

The lie has become almost an art form today. When I was growing up, being branded a liar was almost akin to having leprosy! How things have changed. Nowadays a resourceful creative liar is touted as sly or crafty, but never as vile or repulsive.

The popular use of the lie has exploded in recent years. Has God repealed the ninth commandment? I have never seen so many pathological liars as there are today. When I make that statement, I am not thinking so much about the average man on the street, but of those in the public eye!   Our media reporters, our government officials, even some of the clergy have developed the bald faced lie into a science, and not only that, they now are trying to give the practice a façade of respectability.

One form of untruth is the practice that has been perfected by the news media of selective truth telling.   This practice, while not dealing directly with untruths, uses truth selectively to create an impression that does not truthfully portray the actual situation.   I heard a very amusing story about one of our presidents who was especially disliked by the media.   It is fictitious of   course, but it makes my point.   It seems that this president was fishing with his vice president and his hat blew into the water.   He got out of the boat and walked on the water to retrieve his hat, then walked back across the water and got back into the boat,   the news headline the next day read: "We have positive proof, President XXX cannot swim!"   Selective truth telling at its finest!

We have already covered the practice of selective truth telling to some degree on the subject of war reporting, but they have expanded it into almost every area of the news, especially in the political arena.   It is my belief that the news media has more influence in choosing candidates for election than the voters do. Once the media chooses a candidate, (objectivity be damned), they portray their candidate as a knight in shining armor that can do no harm.   They then report everything negative they can find on the opponents.   This was done most brazenly in the 2008 presidential primaries.   There is no doubt in my mind that if the press had been totally objective in their reporting during that period, the results of both the Democrat and the Republican primaries would have been different.   I am also fairly certain that if it were not for the blatantly skewed reporting of the liberal media after the primaries, Senator John McCain would be the 44th president of these United States.

In the early twentieth century when Edward R. Murrow and Walter Cronkite were bulwarks of the news media, news items were checked, and double checked, prior to airing, and if there was not an overabundance of proof from more than one source, they weren't reported.   If this was still practiced today, Dan Rather would not have been forced into retirement.   The story that attempted to smear President Bush's military record, and became Rather's downfall was published before it was adequately investigated, mainly because it was a story that the powers to be at CBS desperately wanted to be true.

If someone were to ask me what the most important job of the news media is, I would answer that it is twofold. First and foremost, to accurately, without bias, report *all* the important events of the present, and secondly, to archive as accurately as possible the events of the past. In my estimation, the news media of today has reneged on both these tasks, and is concentrating on trying to mold and influence the events of the future!

They seem to have a secondary goal of trying to rewrite the past. There was a documentary series that came out on the television when I was a young man called "You are There". I believe it was narrated by Walter Cronkite. I watched and enjoyed nearly every episode as it was for the most part a summary of recorded historical facts, making use whenever possible of the original on the scene filming. It did not editorialize, and treated our national heroes fairly.

Comparing that series to the historical documentaries of today we come up with apples and oranges. The modern documentaries are more editorial than documentary, are highly opinionated, and skewed toward the extreme socialist left wing agenda of the media. They frequently downplay the achievements of our national heroes, and portray them as having sinister secret agendas rather than love of country, and/or faith in God. By casting aspersions on our founding fathers morality and godliness, they weaken the validity of our constitution, which those forefathers created; a document that they desire to tear apart and recreate to satisfy their own ungodly point of view.

The advent of the internet has empowered modern mankind to spread libel and slander worldwide with practical impunity. While the laws against libel and slander do apply to internet postings, because of their anonymity and their sheer volume, it is practically impossible for the authorities to exercise any control. One can submit postings from any computer, at work, at the neighbors, or even at the public library, under a pseudonym, and it would take months, sometimes years to identify them.   Realizing the impossibility of this task, the authorities have practically thrown in the towel.   They have neither the manpower nor the resources to exercise any semblance of control.   Internet "bloggers" have become a valuable tool for corrupt vitriolic politics, and are operating virtually unchecked.   Knowing that they probably won't get caught, they throw caution to the winds and post unconscionable distortions of the true facts. Their radical postings are extremely detrimental to the democratic process due to their wide distribution.   While our political parties claim no affiliation with these bloggers, (hmmm) it is ludicrous to assume that these bloggers have no affiliation with the political parties!   When the powers to be of these political parties are queried about these blatant fabrications, their usual response is to smile and say: "We have no control over these people.", as they walk away into the sunset.   I believe the majority of these bloggers are actually energetic enthusiastic political, activists, with little or no conscience, and an attitude of "we must win regardless".

A term that I heard one politician use lately to describe a lie is the word "misspoke".   I looked up the word in the dictionary and it listed two meanings.   First, it means to mispronounce a word, and secondly it means to not express oneself clearly.   When someone claims that something happened that really didn't happen, that doesn't fit either of those descriptions.   They didn't misspeak, they lied outright!

I am beginning to get the picture now; we commoners lie while the elite merely misspeak!

This elitist attitude in Washington has led our politicians to devise a double standard, one for them and a different one for us. Guess which one is the most lenient?

I recently, for the first time, visited a web site that keeps track of the "escapades" of our congress.   While I was expecting to see details of some misconduct, (after all that is what that web site reports), I was totally unprepared for what I actually saw.   After a half hour of sordid details of waste fraud and abuse, I was of the same opinion as Mark Twain when he said: "America is the only country without a criminal class, unless you count congress". During that half hour I hadn't even scratched the surface.   There was page after page of exploits, concerning hundreds of members of congress. Some were minor infractions, but most were very serious immoral and often illegal acts. I was not only amazed by the sheer volume of criminal activity that was catalogued there, but also by the fact that about ninety percent of it goes unpunished! I was also quite surprised to find that some members of congress that I considered to be honest and above board were NOT honest and above board!

I logged out clearly convinced that the whole congress with only minor exceptions brazenly considers itself to be above the law.

Quoting from our constitution, article one, section 6: 'The Senators and Representatives shall receive a compensation for their services to be ascertained by law, and paid out of the treasury of the United States. **They shall in all cases, except treason, felony, and breach of the peace, be privileged from arrest during their attendance at the session of their respective houses, and in going to and returning from the same;** and for any speech or debate in either house, they shall not be questioned in any other place." (End quote)

The immunity from arrest in section six was devised to counter the possibility that a number of congressmen might be arrested on trumped up charges in order to render them absent from an important vote on the floor of either house of congress. The rules committees of both houses have expanded the definition and scope of this immunity from arrest beyond what was originally intended to allow serious misconduct to occur without appropriate punishment. Of course, congress has no authority to expand the scope of this clause without a constitutional amendment, but in most cases the liberal courts have upheld their broad interpretation. Members have frequently abused this privilege by using it to interfere with law enforcement investigations, and prosecutorial discovery procedures, thus delaying the solution for long extended periods. These long drawn out legal battles often cause the prosecution to withdraw in disgust. Although they often times flagrantly violate the public trust, and sometimes the public laws, legislators seldom receive more than a slap on the wrist. It is no wonder that their confidence rating by the voting public is down in the teens at present, and has been down to a single digit in the recent past.

The snake oil salesmen of Madison Avenue, (the advertising industry), have perfected the use of the lie and the half-truth to the umpteenth degree. They employ thousands of college graduates who have been trained to skillfully stretch the truth in advertising to its outer limits. They bring a whole new meaning to the terms "consumer beware", and "to boldly go where no man has gone before". The entire industry has become so engulfed in deceitfulness that honesty has become a dirty word in their vocabulary. While they may not be dishonest in the legal sense, (they are usually too smart for that), their methods are so underhanded as to be, at least, morally unjust.

As an example, I know a lady who was stationed in the military here in Texas, and her home was in Indiana. She received a flyer in the mail at her parent's house that stated that she had definitely won ten thousand dollars in cash, and a diamond ring. The only requirement was that she had to collect the prize in person. Thinking that the offer was legitimate, her mother forwarded the flyer to her. As the offer had a time limit, she immediately took leave from the military and drove to Indiana to collect her prize.

When she attempted to collect, she discovered that she had to first sit through a sales presentation on a new real estate development in the area. When she inquired about the prize offer, she was shown the fine print at the bottom of the flyer which read "We reserve the right to substitute a prize of equal value." The substitute prize was a certificate worth ten thousand dollars towards the purchase of a seventy thousand dollar property. The diamond ring she received was of very poor quality, and practically worthless.

The flyer that she received was carefully designed to create a false impression, and in this case it certainly did. Both she and her mom were duped.

The creators of such advertising are counting on the fact that most people will not carefully scrutinize the whole document, but will focus on what they want to see. Everyone wants to be a winner, so they focus on the bold print and have no desire to look for hidden loopholes.   This is one time when it pays to be a pessimist!

Another Madison Avenue practice that has become a public nuisance of epidemic proportions is the telemarketing industry. When the practice began, the telephone lines were inundated with advertisements for everything from airplanes to zebras at all hours of the day, and sometimes at night.   It became so annoying that legislators had to set limits on it, but the limits that could be legally set under the first amendment were inadequate so the industry still flourishes today.   I pay a monthly fee to my telephone provider just to block computer generated telemarketing messages, but they still get through on occasion.   Prior to purchasing this service, I received approximately ten such calls daily!   These were extremely aggravating.   How do you tell a computer to "shut up and get off my line"?

Our government has instituted a "no call" list, and that worked for a while, but the companies involved soon learned that they could generate the calls offshore with immunity, so they are now back in business as before.   The only difference is that now someone in a foreign country is getting paid for what Americans used to do!

Then there is junk mail.   I throw away about five pounds of unopened junk mail weekly.   I live in a city of about thirty seven thousand population, and considering the average family to be three and one half people, that computes to slightly more than ten thousand households throwing away about fifty three thousand pounds of junk mail a week, or nearly twenty six and a quarter tons of wasted paper weekly.   As this is considered a small city, think of the numbers for a city like New York, or Miami!

The postal system has to deliver all this mail, and the city waste disposal has to process it.   This is all done at the consumer's expense.   One might argue that the advertisers pay the postage, but who do you think pays for their advertising budget?   You do when you buy their products!   In this day of "living green", think of the added burden on our national forests caused by the manufacture of all that paper.

In this chapter I have enumerated several dishonest and/or dishonorable practices that are rampant in today's society.   The reason that I include them in this book is to show that although many who indulge in these practices may claim to be Christian, they have a multitude of differing conceptions of who God is, and what is their responsibility to him. While these practices do not directly equate to a revision of man's conception of God, they certainly equate to a revision of God's golden rule of "do unto others as you would have them do unto you". They also relate directly to man's lack of fear of God, and his disdain for God's published moral code.

CHAPTER TEN

BECAUSE THAT WHEN THEY KNEW GOD-

Remember the Bible verses I quoted from the book of Romans at the beginning of this book?

21. Because that, when they knew God, they glorified him not as God, neither were thankful; but became vain in their imaginations, and their foolish heart was darkened.

22. Professing themselves to be wise, they became fools.

23. And changed the glory of the uncorruptible God into an image made like to corruptible man,---

25. Who changed the truth of God into a lie, and worshipped and served the creature more than the creator---

Let's examine these verses one phrase at a time. *Because that, when they knew God,---* I would estimate that ninety nine percent of mankind has some degree of knowledge and/or belief in the existence of God. Their definition of him may be quite different than mine; they may not even have a definition, but may believe him to be some unknown entity that they have no desire to know or understand, but they believe somewhat doubtfully that there may be something or someone out there.

I have never met anyone that I would consider a true atheist. I have met a lot of people who call themselves atheists, but under closer examination, I find that they do in fact believe in God, they just don't want anything to do with him. Most people who call themselves atheists are quick to let you know that they are anti-God. How can you be anti something that doesn't exist? The more radical ones openly campaign against God and his principles. Doesn't that seem a little bizarre to you, to campaign against something that you claim doesn't exist? Seems like a complete waste of time and energy to me!

Suppose you saw me in the middle of an empty parking lot, swinging an axe. Your first reaction would be to ask, "What are you doing?" To which I would reply, "I am chopping down a tree." "But there is no tree."

"I know," as I continue swinging the axe. Your next reaction would probably be to call 911!

A wise man once said: "If there were no God, man would of necessity invent one." An age old two-fold question has been, where did I come from, How did I become what I am? As I mentioned in our discussion of evolution versus divine creation, there had to be some supernatural eternal force responsible for the start of the process in either case. I believe that man has recognized the existence of this force from day one. Mankind, in his quest for knowledge, has a need for everything to be identified, catalogued, and ordered. The easiest way for him to identify this force was to give it a name and a face. All the great societies of the past, the Egyptians, the Medo-Persians, the Greeks, and the Romans to name a few, invented multiple personalities in the form of a family of gods.

These gods were almost always considered to be unique to the particular society that invented them. These gods were invented not only to explain man's origin and destiny, but quite often were used as a tool to maintain order and control. The phrase "God said" carried a lot more weight than the phrase "The King said". These gods were carefully tailored to legitimize a particular life style. Warlike nations would conjure up gods of war, while peace loving nations had gods of love and compassion, licentious societies had fertility gods. As they were mythological, their effect on the society they served was purely philosophical rather than substantial. Interpreting the will of these gods was the responsibility of a handful of priests, soothsayers, and mediums, who often used their position for personal advantage. As each of these societies declined into oblivion, their gods went with them. Their invented gods were powerless to rescue them.

If we, as a nation today re-invent our God, and change our definition of him into something that he is not, as many desire to do, we will join all those other societies on the discard heap of time.

We as Americans must maintain the absolute purity, integrity, and deity of the God of the Bible if we are to endure as a people. I firmly believe that America was one of two nations that were pre-ordained of God for a special purpose, Israel being the other. Israel was chosen by God to carry his word to the world, and most importantly to provide the world with a savior. America was chosen to be the big brother, protector of the tiny nation. If we continue on the immoral path down which we are headed, I fear that God will regret at least one of his choices!

The God of Christianity differs from these former gods in three ways. First, he has stood the test of time. While the other gods have come and gone, the God of the Bible remains eternal. These former gods receive no mention today, except in mythological terms in the past tense, while our God has been active in the recorded history of man for as long as history has been recorded.

A very unique difference between those made up gods of the past and our God, is the fact that he was more often rejected than accepted by the Israelite nation. As I said before, the other gods were tailor made to fit the society that invented them, but not so our God. If he was merely a fictional creation of the minds of the Israelites, then he would have been given a nature that more closely conformed to their aspirations and lifestyle, and they would have fervently believed in and defended his existence just as the other nations did their gods. Why would a nation create a god whose standards of conduct were in almost constant conflict with their lifestyle? Of course, they would not. Therefore, the premise that the God of the Bible was just another created deity, conjured up by the Israelite nation seems highly unlikely.

Secondly, he does not embrace only one group or nationality, but is the God of the whole universe. Some of you may disagree, having the idea that he is partial to the nation of Israel, and you would be correct in part, but God chose Israel basically for two reasons, as I have already stated, one, to publish his word, and two, to provide the world with a savior. The nation of Israel has suffered extremes of prejudice and envy simply because of their special relationship to God. In order that they might accomplish what God has purposed that they do, God has miraculously maintained the nation of Israel through hardships that no other nation has experienced, but his love for his creation encompasses the whole of it, not just the nation of Israel.

Thirdly, our God interacts with his creation. Ask any born again Christian and they will tell you that they can feel the presence of God in their daily lives in a very real way. His presence is especially evident whenever Christian people gather together and their thoughts and conversation turn to him. I can find no record where any of these other gods interacted in any way.

On a lighter note, why is it that whenever something pleasant happens it is classified as good luck, but a tragic storm is called an "act of God"? But seriously, if you credit him for the storm, are you not acknowledging his existence? Did you know that "act of God" is a legally recognized term that holds importance in some judicial decisions? I am surprised that the ACLU has not tried to have the term removed from the legal vocabulary. I assume it is because the use of the term does not usually refer to God favorably, instead it usually points to him as a destructive force, and to them that is advantageous to their agenda. On the one hand, you must never, in the public forum, mention, portray, or even recognize the righteous, benevolent, loving, God of the Bible, but it is OK to blame him for earthquakes, violent storms, the occasional flat tire, and that painful corn on your little toe!

Instances have been recorded of unexplained healings brought about by prayer. One such incident happened to me in 1982. Prior to that time, during my last two years in the military, (1976-78) I suffered bouts of excruciating back pain to the extent that I could not move at times. On three separate occasions I had to be transported to the hospital in an ambulance. The doctors treated the symptoms, bringing temporary relief, but the pain kept coming back. When I retired from the military in 1978, my life was much less physical, and I was able to "baby" my back somewhat, but I still had bouts of pain from time to time. This pain would usually come at a time when I was under unusual mental stress, but it was sometimes, although less frequently, caused by physical activity. On Memorial Day week-end of 1982, I was working on the road for a defense contractor in San Antonio Texas and I had driven home for a visit. That Sunday afternoon, I had a bout of back pain that nearly crippled me.

Knowing that I had to be at work Tuesday morning, (I could barely walk), I shuffled to my vehicle and drove myself to the military hospital at Fort Hood Texas. As soon as I got to the hospital, I felt very uneasy about being there. I had to wait in a long line to get my records, and there was a young woman in front of me with a baby on her arm that was pink all over with fever. Standing there in line, with unrelenting pain, I felt more and more uncomfortable about the whole situation, and when the baby started to vomit, I said to myself "that's it, I'm out of here." After spending twenty years in the military, I was used to standing in lines, and normally it would not bother me, but this time it was totally different. I just felt that I was doing the wrong thing. I realized later that God wanted to help me, but I was interfering with his plan. As quickly as I could, I shuffled out to the car and drove home.

When I opened the car door, I could not stand so I crawled on my hands and knees to the front door and into my bedroom where I prayed what was probably the most stupid prayer I have ever uttered. My exact words were: "God, IF YOU CAN, please take away this pain." It was a prayer of acute desperation. I had just accepted Christ as my savior six months prior, and I was still a baby Christian. I believe God said "Son, you need a lesson in faith!" A warmth came over me, the pain all but went away, and I lay down in my bed and slept a most peaceful sleep for the first time in several days. When I awoke, it was gone, never to return to this day. I will never again have even the slightest doubt in God's ability to heal the human body.

I have witnessed several such healings, and heard testimony of many others. I know that some of you have heard about fake healing services with hidden microphones and "ringers" planted in the crowds, and I must admit that this does take place from time to time, but not as often as the real thing. A few charlatans are giving the rest of us a bad name! I also know of other healings that took place just as mine did with no preacher, no microphones, no ringers, just me and God!

Modern man would have us believe that this is not the power of God, but just mind over matter, or some natural cause, but I know what I know! I know that it was the awesome power of God that healed me! When modern man tries to deny that power, he is trying to make God less than he is, by redefining his capabilities.

Looking on the dark side, there is a very real spirit world, inhabited by demonic spirits whose only purpose is to antagonize and contaminate God's creation. I was present at an exorcism that was performed on a lady whom I knew pretty well. She would seldom attend a local church, but if a TV preacher was conducting a service anywhere within two hundred miles, she would attend. She seemed very much to me to be enthralled more with the messengers than with their messages. Church to her was just a form of exotic entertainment. She was entrapped in a snare that satan has used effectively on a great many "wanna-be" Christians.

When the demon was confronted, it spoke with a deep, guttural voice that was definitely not hers. I recall the demon saying: "you can't have her, she's mine. Her grandmother gave her to me." I also remember the demon saying: "I hate her for bringing me to church. She's always bringing me to church, I hate church." There were other things said by this demon spirit, but those are the only words I can remember verbatim.

The point I am trying to make is this, if this dark or devils side of the spirit world exists, then by association, the bright side, or God's side must exist also. There are a lot of people who are not Christians who believe in this dark side of the spirit world, they believe in the devil and demons, in witchcraft, voodoo, and mojo, but I say to them that you really can't have one without the other, they come as a set.

In this segment, I have recorded examples of events in my own life that lead me to positively believe in the God the Bible. I find it very hard to believe that there is any individual who has reached the age of accountability that has not at least heard of similar events that would suggest that God is real.

God is not elusive; he does not hide from mankind. While he cannot have direct contact with mankind due to the sinful nature of man, He makes his presence known through intermediaries. God chooses pastors, evangelists, and various other church officers to administer his word, his perfect love, and his benevolence to his creation.

Since the advent of Christ's crucifixion and resurrection, God's primary intermediary is the Holy Ghost, the third person of the triune Godhead. I used to wonder how the Holy Ghost, an integral part of the person of God, could co-habit with mankind, as God cannot co-exist with sin, and one day God gave me the answer. The Holy Ghost has no part in judgment. His purpose is to inhabit the consciences of all humankind, and cause each of them to consider their responsibility and relationship to God, their creator. It is the Holy Ghost that causes us to realize our sinful nature, and our need for salvation from that sinful state.

We read in Romans 1:19&20: *Because that which may be known of God is manifest in them; for God hath showed it unto them. For the invisible things of him from the creation of the world are clearly seen, being understood by the things that are made, even his eternal power and Godhead: so that they are without excuse.*

Is there evidence that God exists? Absolutely! While God himself is physically invisible to mankind, his works of interaction with his creation are not. Miracles of healings and other blessings that can only be described as supernatural, (defying the laws of nature), the amazing order of the universe, and the harmony of life where each species fits into a master plan of mutual benefit, one to another, are plainly evident, and point emphatically to a single master plan by a sole creator. His name is Jehovah God.

CHAPTER ELEVEN

they glorified him not as God—

One question I would like to ask God when I eventually come face to face with him is, "why did you give man an ego?"

I recall watching Dr. Charles Stanley preaching on the TV and he asked the question, "What part of the body is most responsible for keeping a person from going to heaven?" He then gave several answers: "Some may say the eye, but that is not it; some may say the tongue, but that is not it; some may say the hand, but that is not it; some may say the foot, but that is not it." He then tapped the back of his knee with his hand and said: "This is it because it can't do this." He then knelt on the floor as if in prayer. I may have paraphrased his wording somewhat, and if I did I apologize, but you get the picture. Man's reluctance to submit to any authority higher than himself has stood between him and God tragically more often than not. That reluctance is the main motive for mankind's current trend of trying to bring God down to his own level, to reinvent God. God's standards of conduct are far above even what the strongest, most moral man could possibly achieve, so by attempting to redefine and relax God's standards, mankind eases his conscience.

If God's standards are so high as to be unattainable, then how can he expect man to comply with them? The answer is, he DOESN'T! When God initially gave man the original commandments, laws, and ordinances in the Old Testament, he knew full well that man could not meet their requirements. God gave them to show man that his conduct did not meet God's established standard, and therefore man stood in need of an intermediary. That is why at the same time that he gave man the law, he defined a system of temple worship and sacrifice that would bring man back in right standing with God in spite of man's penchant for sin.   This system of sacrifice culminated in the ultimate sacrifice of Jesus Christ on the cross of Calvary.   When Jesus willingly gave his life on the cross at Calvary, the condemnation for man's sins was forever negated.   All that God requires of man is that he admit to himself and God that without his acceptance of that sacrifice, he would be condemned to a sinners fate.

Because of his pride, it is hard for modern man to admit to his mistakes.   As man becomes more and more intellectual, his self esteem grows and grows.   It grows to the point that he is much less willing to admit his failures in his relationship with his creator.   In his eyes, he is good enough that God should be willing to except him as he is, and it is wrong in his estimation for God to require him to humble himself.   Be that as it may, the formula for salvation is defined by God, with no assistance either needed or desired from mankind, and it is non-negotiable.   Psalm 119, verse 89 reads: *O Lord, thy word is settled in heaven.*   It is really quite simple; the only way to get into heaven is from a kneeling position!   If you can't call Jesus Lord, he can't be your savior!

Neither were thankful

I heard a cute little story that fits here perfectly.   It seems that a business man was about to be late for an appointment, and he was searching frantically for a parking place.   He prayed, "Lord, if you will find me a parking place next to the building, I will go to church every Sunday."   Suddenly a parking place opened up right in front of the door.   As the other car was pulling away he said: "Never mind, I found one."

Actually, if everyone were completely satisfied all the time, society would stagnate.   Dissatisfaction breeds discovery; discovery breeds progress, so a little constructive discontent is healthy.   Instead of the constructive discontent I would like to address the negativism that is displayed by a large group of modern day whiners, many of whom are Christians.   Some people seem to have a penchant for crying and complaining about every little thing.   You know, the kind of people that if you gave them a one hundred dollar bill with no strings attached, they would complain that it wasn't two fifties. I am talking about those hapless individuals who believe that they are constantly being short changed by the world around them, and more incredibly, they believe they are being shortchanged by God.

More and more, I hear Christians ask why God let certain things happen, or why he doesn't act in the way they believe he should.

James chapter four, verse two and three says *"ye have not because ye ask not. Ye ask and ye receive not, because ye ask amiss, that ye may consume it upon your lusts."*

Here's how most people pray: "God, I have this terrible problem; here is the way I desire to have this problem resolved; now make MY solution happen, Amen!" You don't need God, you need a do it yourself handbook on how to be your own god! If the current trend continues, I suspect someone will probably write one!

We often ask for ground beef when God has "T" bone in mind. I once heard a story that illustrates this point vividly. There was a European immigrant who scrimped and saved just enough money for passage on an ocean liner to New York, and knowing that the trip would take twelve days, he brought some bread and sausage aboard, which he hid under the cover of one of the life boats. While the other passengers dined sumptuously in the dining room, he would sneak out to the life boat for a meager meal. The bread got a little stale, and the sausage got a little dry, but he survived the ordeal. When he got to New York, a friend who had previously made the same trip met him at the pier and asked him about his trip. He told his friend that he was kind of hungry because he had to survive on his meager fare as he did not have the money for the dining room, to which his friend replied "Didn't you know that the price of the meals was included in the ticket?" Alas, if he had only went to the master of the ship!

Nearly all the things that dissatisfy us are our own fault. We are sometimes ignorant of God's providence, or we may be disobedient to his will, or for one reason or another we just fail to ask. When we do ask, we sometimes pray selfish prayers, not stopping to consider the consequences of our request. Some years back, God taught me a lesson about selfish prayers. My wife was going through her midlife crisis which sometimes resulted in bouts of anger, whenever she had a bad hair day. On my way home from work, I took to praying that there would be peace in my home when I came in the door. After a few days of this, a little voice spoke to me in the recesses of my mind saying "Instead of praying on the way home that YOU will have peace, why don't you pray in the morning before you go to work that SHE will have a good day?" You know what? It worked!

In first Thessalonians, chapter five, and verse seventeen we read: "Pray without ceasing". I don't believe that God expects us to walk around on our knees, with our eyes closed, and hands clasped in front of our chest in the traditional posture of prayer; that would be difficult to say the least, but we should be subconsciously communicating with him at all times.

We are a constantly communicating people with each other, why not with God? The use of cellular phones has become so popular as to become a nuisance at times. More than once, I have been walking down the aisle in the supermarket and someone right next to me would say something that I thought was directed toward me, and I would answer them, only to receive a strange look, and I would then note that they had a cell phone to their ear. What an embarrassing moment! Some people are talking on their cell phone constantly. Maybe God ought to provide each of us with a cell phone, connected constantly to heaven so that we would stay in contact with him at all times as we should. (Actually, he does, it's called the Holy Ghost network, but he gets a lot of busy signals from our end.) If we were in constant contact, and following his directions, our number of complaints would rapidly decrease to zero.

Instead of being thankful that God has given him dominion over all creation, man chooses rather to whine and complain. He is forever questioning God's actions and motives. While some of these questions are just normal curiosity, (I myself would like to know why he made the skunk and poison ivy, each with which I have had a very unpleasant experience), but other questions are of a far more serious nature. I cannot count the number of times I have heard someone ask why God let certain events happen, or perhaps the most commonly asked question of all, why did God let mama die?

There are two schools of thought among Christians concerning God's interaction in our lives. One belief is that from the moment one becomes a Christian, God controls nearly every aspect of their life, and that every thing that happens to them, whether good or bad, is part of a master plan for their lives. Others believe that God allows us a large degree of freedom to choose the direction that we will follow, and even though our choices may be near tragic at times, he will not interfere unless we ask him to. I strongly agree with the latter school of thought.

The first school of thought allows us to blame God for our problems, and nearly all the complaints against God come from those people who maintain that belief. They try to rationalize their behavior by saying that God must have a reason for their life to turn out the way it has. This is a cop-out that is used to excuse spiritual failure! This rationale has been used to cover a multitude of sins, but I have news for those who attempt to use it, Unconfessed sin is unforgiven sin! In the book of first John, chapter one, verse nine we read:

If we confess our sins, he is faithful and just to forgive us our sins, and cleanse us from all unrighteousness. (Emphasis on "if") I say again, unconfessed sin is unforgiven sin!

The second school of thought places the blame squarely where it belongs, on ourselves. This requires us to accept responsibility for our sins, and to deal with them as God has decreed that we should. The only way I can receive reconciliation for my sins is to confess them to God and accept his forgiveness. To claim that God is responsible for the way I sometimes act, borders on blasphemy!

The ways that we as individuals act and the events that occur in our lives are for the most part the results of our own imperfect choices. Of course, God is always there to call upon when we need him, but most of us egotistically desire to go it on our own, and not bother God with our troubles. We should seek his guidance in everything we do, but sadly, most of us don't. This attitude of "I can handle it on my own" has caused untold misery to fall upon

God's children.   We wait until the noose begins to tighten, and then pray frantically for His intervention.

Some people claim that the miserable state of their existence is all part of "God's plan", rather than admitting their mistakes and seeking his help in rectifying them.   They are partakers of that first school of thought that God is in control of every waking moment. God has never, nor will he ever purposely inflict undue pain and suffering on his people.   The pain and suffering that we feel are the direct results of the way we live.   I have heard so many people say "God intended for me to be poor."   No. you are poor because you have claimed it, and don't have the gumption to change it.   You are just using God as an excuse.   "God intended for me to have lung cancer."   No, you just smoked one too many cigarettes.

Getting back to "Why did God let Mama die?" I have heard a lot of Christians, including the majority of the preachers that I know, espouse the idea that God has picked a particular date for each individual to die.   I am probably of a minority opinion, but I don't believe that.   While I am absolutely certain that God knows the exact date, minute, and second that we are going to die before we are even born, there is a difference between him knowing, and choosing.   I believe the date that we die is determined by the choices we make in life.   There is just no way I can believe that it is God's will for a certain man to become an alcoholic and die at thirty five of sclerosis of the liver.   His untimely death would be a direct result of his own choice to drink in excess.   What if the same man made a decision at an early age to never touch alcohol; would he still die of the same disease at the same age?   I think not.   I heard a story about a man who was asked if he would like to know the exact moment that he would die, and he replied "No, I would rather know the place where I would die."

"Why would you want to know that?"

"Because I would never go there!"

It is hard for most folks to comprehend that God knows everyone's future, even the most tragic ones, to the minutest detail, and yet does nothing to interfere.   God need only speak it, and mankind would never again have a free choice in anything.   Man would become robotic, and always do the right thing at the right time in the right place. Why doesn't God do that?

I have an electric drill in my workshop. It is completely predictable, whenever I plug it in to the wall and pull the trigger, it does exactly what it is supposed to do. While that drill has assisted me in many projects and I have been pleased with its performance, I could never have a loving relationship with that drill, nor it with me; get the picture? God must allow man to have free choices in the affairs of his life, so that he can CHOOSE to have an intimate relationship with God.

There is a group of Christians that I call the "name it and claim it crowd". They seem to have a very strange notion of who God is and how their relationship with him ought to develop. They operate under the premise that because God has made certain promises in his word, that man can DEMAND that God honor these promises. These promises deal with blessings such as healing, financial prosperity, and divine protection from danger to name a few. What they are leaving out of the equation is the fact that God has placed conditions on these promises. Going back to the book of Isaiah, chapter one, the three verses that I quoted in a previous chapter,

18. Come now, let us reason together, saith the Lord: though your sins be as scarlet, they shall be as white as snow; though they be red like crimson, they shall be as wool.

19. If ye be willing and obedient, ye shall eat the good of the land:

20. But if ye refuse and rebel. Ye shall be devoured with the sword, for the mouth of the Lord hath spoken it.

Notice that very important word "if" is in there twice. Salvation is the only promise of God that is totally free, with no preconditions, except for repentance. All the other promises are contingent on us being "willing and obedient", if we would "eat the good of the land."

Now who is to judge whether I am willing and obedient?

Do you know anyone who could confidently stand before God and declare: "I have been willing and obedient and therefore you must give me of the good of the land."? In the book of first John, 1:8 if we say that we have no sin, we deceive ourselves, and the truth is not in us.

It seems to me that if I say that I am willing and obedient, that is the same as saying I have no sin, and that makes me a liar!

Can you picture an accused individual striding up to the judge in court and saying: "I have already judged myself to be innocent so now you have to let me go."?

I was once invited by a co-worker to a revival at his church. When he told me about the evangelist, I was taken aback. It seems that this evangelist was once the bodyguard for one of the most outspoken media preachers of this "name it and claim it" crowd. I once heard this media preacher state that whenever he got on an airplane to fly someplace that he claimed the airplane in the name of Jesus, so he knew that nothing could go wrong. If he had so much faith in God's providence and protection, why did he feel the need for a bodyguard? I immediately thought to myself, "Oh ye of little faith!" Maybe his guardian angel was on an extended vacation or something. In any event, it seems he wasn't too good at practicing what he preached.

These people are not serving God; they are demanding that God serve them! They are trying to change God into a mere servant!

CHAPTER TWELVE

But became vain in their imaginations

My dictionary gives three meanings for the word vain, (1) excessively proud (2) unsuccessful (3) empty of substance. I believe the latter definition is the intended meaning in this phrase, much the same as King Solomon, in the book of Ecclesiastes describes the hollowness of the joys of worldly living as "all is vanity."

It is not enough for man to know that God exists. He wants to know what God looks like so he conjures up a mental picture. With practically no clues to go by, he must, for the most part, use his imagination.

As an example, I know that most of us have at one time or another heard personalities on the radio that intrigued us. As we listen to their voice, which is the only clue to their identity that we have, we begin to build an image in our mind of what we suppose they look like. It is human nature to do this. This image is for the most part, a product of our imagination, and we do the same thing with God.

I heard a cute little story that may or may not be true, but it illustrates what I am writing about.

A Sunday school class of eight year olds was given a task for each student to draw a character of their choosing from the Bible. When all but one of the students was finished, the teacher went to each one and asked them who they had drawn. One drew Jonah in the whale, another drew Joseph and his coat of many colors, still another drew Moses parting the waters, Etc. When she came to the last little girl, who was still intensely working on her drawing she asked, "And who are you drawing?"
"I am drawing God."

"But nobody knows what God looks like."

"They will in a minute!"

The image that we conjure up becomes very real to us, just as it did to that little eight year old girl, but that does not mean that it is accurate. In almost every case, it is not. Going back to the radio personalities, I have been quite astonished at times to see their picture in the media, or see them on television, and the image that I had developed in my mind didn't even come close!

Modern man has developed a mental image of God that is less majestic, less stately, and less grand in order to bring God down to man's level. He has attempted to pollute the perfect character of God by attributing to him traits that are unmistakably human.

There is a modern theory being taught in some religious curriculum today that God made a series of mistakes and corrections in his relationship to man. This negates the infallibility of God, and opens his flawlessness to criticism. This theory purports that God did not know that Adam would sin in the garden; that the people would rebel during the exodus from Egypt; that they would turn to idolatry when they reached the Promised Land; and in each case he had to take corrective measures. God had foreknowledge of every little detail of everyone's life before he began creation. He even knows the next time you will sneeze! You may wonder why he didn't do something in the beginning to prevent the sin and apostasy before they happened, but if he did, then he would be interfering with man's free choice, a necessary, integral part of the creator/creation relationship. For you Star Trek fans out there, it is much the same as the "Prime directive."

I have met a lot of people in this world who can describe God to a "T". They know all there is to know about him and his message to mankind and they are extremely vocal in letting us know that. There is only one problem; they have little or no idea what they are talking about. I call them the "Archie Bunkers" of this world. Most of you who have reached my age will remember old Archie from the TV series "All in the Family". Whenever Archie used the phrase "the good book says", you could be assured that a distortion of God's word was coming. These people either know God's word, and purposely distort it to suit their own purpose, or they have little or no knowledge and fill in the blank spaces from their imagination. Their wild excursions into the twilight zone result in weird descriptions of God's person and purpose. These self proclaimed "Bible experts" vigorously and emphatically defend their views, but one thing I have observed in my sixty plus years is this: the person with the weakest argument invariably argues the loudest!

There is a man that I know with whom I have occasional contact, who likes to argue about the Bible. To my knowledge this man does not own a Bible, and from our conversations I can tell that he has a very limited knowledge of God's true word. He tends to favor abstract and bizarre interpretations over traditional doctrines.

On several occasions I have shown him what the Bible actually says about some particular point where he had a contrary view, and he would usually counter with: "Reverend so and so said that on TV, and he must know what he is talking about." It seems that his only contact with the word of God is second hand and often tainted by vain imagination.

THE DOCTRINES OF MEN!

Jesus said in Mark 7:7 *Howbeit in vain do they worship me, teaching for doctrines the commandments of men.*

This man is willing to reject the word of God in favor of what some preacher said on TV.

I am not trying to say that all TV preachers preach the doctrines of men. Perhaps he is just listening to the wrong preachers, or he is misunderstanding what these preachers are trying to say, or he may be purposely taking them out of context, but the end result is the same. This man has a very distorted view of who God is and what his message to mankind proclaims. I fear that he is not an isolated case, but that there are millions like him in our society today, and that their numbers are growing at an alarming rate.

And their foolish heart was darkened

Throughout the Bible darkness represents evil while light represents goodness. The phrase "their foolish heart" represents the collective conscience of mankind.

While it is wrong to categorize every single person as coming from the same mold, there are certain changing trends in the attitudes and behavior of society as a whole that are plainly evident and represent a distinct change in direction. This entire book is all about just such a trend that is developing at present.

Up until the mid nineteenth century our nation was basically "one nation, under God". The conscience of our nation was for the most part formed of Godly principals, and even those who did not subscribe, passively tolerated and even appreciated Godly living.

In the aftermath of the civil war, we seemed to have turned a corner. The opening of the west to settlement, and the industrial revolution, with their resultant affluence bred graft and corruption at an alarming rate. Godly principals took a back seat to personal self interests.

This trend was temporarily interrupted by two world wars when the majority of the populace put self interests aside for a while, but the quest was not forgotten. After the wars the trend continued.

This trend of late seems to have shifted into overdrive. It is my belief that the devil, knowing that his time is short, is trying to cause as much havoc as possible before he is stripped of his ability to do so. He has entangled himself in our national psyche with a death grip.

Up until the last three or four decades, ungodly behavior was mostly frowned upon by the majority, but then we seemed to have turned another corner. Suddenly in almost every facet of our lifestyle, position became synonymous with privilege, the higher the position, the greater the privilege to sin with virtual impunity. There seems to be a growing disgust for Christianity among our leaders. There is a concerted effort by most of them to distance themselves from any obligation to recognize godly precepts of behavior, and to replace them with the constantly worsening doctrines of men. Our collective national conscience (our foolish heart) is slowly darkening. The light has not gone completely out, but it sure is growing dim!

True wisdom is always seasoned with humility. You will never hear a truly wise person say "I am wise", as they are saying in this passage (professing themselves). True wisdom will always manifest itself; it does not have to be professed.

I believe that modern man has mistaken intelligence for wisdom. There is a difference. Intelligence is static, while wisdom is active. I would define wisdom as the effective use of intelligence. In order for raw intelligence to be useful, it must be combined with good common sense, and then employed in such a manner as to be beneficial to the user. Mankind today seems to place a great value on, and take pride in, the collection of intelligence, while only casually considering what it might be used for. Through technology and the instant access to information through the internet, the availability of intelligence has increased dramatically in recent years. Sadly, mans capability to use this new found intelligence wisely, has not. I want to cite two cases. In each of these cases mankind used his "intelligence" to attempt to improve God's natural order of existence.

First, will be the importation of the African honey bee. As a native Texan, I am keenly aware of the debacle created by this foolish act. I personally witnessed a swarm of these bees at a National Guard airbase in San Antonio. These bees swarmed on a four foot piece of chain that was used to tie down a helicopter. The swarm was about one foot in diameter surrounding the entire length of the chain.

All operations were ceased, and personnel were cautioned to stay indoors until the animal control people arrived. Fortunately, the animal control people were quickly on the scene, "smoked" the bees, and vacuumed them up before they could do any harm. This was not always the case. During the bees' migration from south to North America, there have been numerous instances where they have caused serious injury and sometimes death to animals and humans alike. The importation of this bee was an unwise use of man's intelligence. While man was aware of the highly aggressive nature of this bee, he wrongly assumed that he could control this aggressiveness. He was wrong!

The second case I want to cite concerns an isolated island on a lake in Minnesota. This island contained a moose herd and a pack of wolves. Because of the distance to shore from all sides of the island, these animals remained isolated there. Someone in the wildlife management service got the bright idea that if they would trap the wolves and remove them from the island that the moose herd should increase, so this was done.

Imagine their embarrassment when after a couple of years, they discovered that the moose herd was decreasing in numbers! They discovered that the wolf pack had been selectively "culling" the moose herd by devouring the old and weak animals, thus reserving the limited supply of food for the healthy animals that were able to produce offspring. (They brought the wolves back!)

It is sacrilege for mankind to assume that he can improve on God's work, but modern man frequently makes that assumption, invariably with disastrous results.

What I consider the most sacrilegious act of "foolish wisdom" is the current trend by the secular elite of academia to correct God's word. There is an ever growing company of scholars, some who profess to be Christians, who believe that the original writers of the Bible were lowly uneducated men, who were brainwashed by the religious leaders of their day, and they did not fully understand what they were writing. They disregard the fact that every single word of the Bible was inspired by God himself. Those men, chosen by God, who wrote down the words of the Bible, were not relying on their own intelligence, but were inspired by the wisdom, knowledge, and intelligence of God!

While there is a loosely concerted effort by these so called wise men of today to bring about change, they propose a myriad of opposing views. It seems that the only thing they can agree upon is their erroneous premise that the word of God is inaccurate, but when it comes to correcting it, they all head in different directions. Their offerings serve to spread confusion rather than clarification, and we all know who the Bible says is the author of confusion, old satan himself! While I doubt that any of these men are purposely serving the devil, they are subconsciously doing his bidding nevertheless! They are serving up doubt and confusion in the minds of all mankind.

CHAPTER THIRTEEN

Who changed the glory of the uncorruptible God—

The absolute majesty and splendor of God have been held in extreme awe and wonder by mankind for centuries. Only of late has man decided to dishonor his obligation to revere God.

Before the invention of the printing press, copies of scriptures were laboriously written by hand. There were selected men called scribes, who were given a place in the temple, whose life's work was to produce these copies. These men held God in such awe and reverence that whenever they came to a place in the scripture where they had to write God's name, they would stop, and go through a ritual of physical and spiritual cleansing before they would dare take quill in hand and write his name. If his name occurred more than once in a scripture, they would go through the same ritual each time.

Most people today would say "that is ridiculous." That is my point exactly! Most people today, including many Christians fail to afford God the reverence he deserves. Most people today observe higher protocols with the boss at work than they do with God!

One pet peeve that I have is irreverent behavior in the church sanctuary.

Leviticus 19:30 *Ye shall keep my Sabbaths, and reverence my sanctuary: I am the Lord.*

I recall when I was just a lad going to church with my Dad and Mom; once we went through the doors into the sanctuary I was to sit down, be quiet, and remain there until church was over. It wasn't long before I discovered one of the reasons why my Mom always wore flat shoes to church; they made a perfect paddle!

The entire congregation was quiet and somber as we waited for the service to begin. An aura of reverence permeated the whole building. Conversations were postponed until church was over and the people were outside. No one was moving around or talking, not even children. It was a quiet time to reflect, to pray, to prepare.

Contrast that with the typical service of today. Church bells are illegal in many cities, so the song leader has to shout at the beginning of the service in order to be heard over the chatter of multiple conversations. This chatter slowly abates until it stops somewhere near the middle of the opening prayer; parents are chasing toddlers up and down the aisles; older children rather than sit with their families, sit with their friends so they can talk throughout the service; cell phones (which, by the way, have an "off" switch) frequently interrupt the service; people bring sodas and bottled water into the sanctuary, sometime even snacks; and during the service it seems that over half the members of the congregation have a Sunday morning bladder problem!

The way we conduct ourselves in HIS sanctuary is not only sometimes insulting to God, but it can be a very real detriment to effective evangelism. A case in point happened in a church where I once pastored.

There was a couple who were church members but they seldom attended services. They expressed a strong concern about how some of the children acted in church as the main reason for their lack of attendance. They were convinced to try one more time, and the next Sunday night they arrived a little early and were sitting in their car in the parking lot.

Two of our young teen boys were outside, kicking a soccer ball around. Just as I came outside to tell them to stop, one of the boys kicked the ball and it landed on the hood of this couples car. I watched in disgust as they backed up and drove away!

When church started, I had those two boys bring two folding chairs and set them down front facing the congregation. I reminded everyone that these two chairs represented the couple who would be sitting in church if they had not been assaulted by a soccer ball!

While this incident did not actually occur inside the sanctuary, it reinforced that couples discontent with what did go on inside to the extent that they turned and drove away.

Remember when Moses came into contact with God in the story of the burning bush? God said "take off your shoes Moses, you are standing on hallowed ground." Whenever we come in contact with the presence of God, that place becomes hallowed ground. Our present point of contact with his presence is the sanctuary.

What would you think if I came to your house and was constantly carrying on a conversation with my wife, ignoring you in the process; allowing my children to run all over the house; and allowing them to lie down on your sofa with their dirty shoes on? If I was to take out a fingernail clipper and proceed to clip my fingernails all over your carpet? If I took out a wad of gum that I had been chewing and stuck it under your coffee table? If one of my children picked up a book that was on the coffee table and began to scribble all over its pages? It seems that some of us expect God to accept such behavior. Words can barely describe my disgust at such irreverence; it seems God is more tolerant than I would be!

Using God's name in vain in the form of profanity is commonplace today, even in mixed company. I once read a little saying in the reader's digest that I thought was worth remembering, and I feel compelled to quote it here. "Profanity is the feeble attempt of an illiterate mind to express itself." Not only is it illiterate, but insulting to God. One strict rule of political correctness is that racial epithets should never be used in public conversation; however the degradation of the name of God seems to be wholly acceptable. Where are the proponents of political correctness in that case?

Into an image like to corruptible man.

Uncorruptible God-corruptible man. One of the most degrading experiences of life is to dwell constantly in the shadow of perfection. There are two ways for man to handle this dilemma. He can elevate himself to the same standard of perfection which is the honorable way to go, or he can attempt to malign the perfection in an effort to bring it down to his level of imperfection.

Modern secular man has chosen the latter method.

Perfection that is acceptable to God is called righteousness. My dictionary describes the word as: "strictly observant of morality: always behaving according to a religious or moral code." Note the use of the word "always". This denotes that righteousness is an absolute. A degree of righteousness does not qualify.

Modern man, for the most part, reluctantly recognizes that God is the author of our moral code of conduct, but instead of accepting the blame for his own frequent failures to comply with the code, he chooses to blame God for setting the bar too high. By doing this, man feels that he can lower the bar himself, and become his own judge of his moral conduct. This results in a false sense of self righteousness that falls short of God's requirements. A growing number of people who profess to be Christians are falling into this practice.

Another area where man falls short of God's requirements is what I call "comparison righteousness," where the individual compares himself to those around him. Using his over-inflated ego, and his biased rationale, he can usually come up with one hundred and one reasons why he is better morally than they are, so God must be proud of him. NOT!

The grandest efforts of mankind to achieve righteousness on his own, are feeble at best in God's eyes, and fall far short of his requirements. That is why God allowed his only begotten son, Jesus Christ to die on the cross, thus bearing all the guilt and punishment that was due mankind. Christ became God in human form, lived a truly righteous life, was guilty of nothing, and therefore had no sin debt to pay. His personal sacrifice, an act of perfect love, became payment in full for the total sin obligation of mankind. To reject that act of love, in prideful self righteousness condemns one to hell in the eternal lake of fire.

The current trend in man's thinking is toward intellectual realism. This line of thinking rejects the concept of divine nature as implausible. By replacing the divine nature with human qualities, God becomes more palatable to the mind of man. The more radical elements of our modern society are engaged in a virulent campaign to "defrock" God and his son Jesus Christ by projecting human qualities on them, and by questioning their teachings, and motives. Their brazenness is only exceeded by their foolishness in attempting to do so!

CHAPTER FOURTEEN

Who changed the truth of God into a lie

While the truth of God encompasses much more than just the Bible, I have already adequately covered man's attempts to change the other aspects of God's truth, so in this section I will concentrate on man's attempts to discredit or change the Bible.

There have been numerous attempts of late in the media, even in the religious media, to bring up spectacular or bizarre interpretations of God's word.   These interpretations and prophesies are conjured up in the minds of men, often accompanied by the claim that they were received in a revelation that came directly from God.   Any offering from these men that radically revises or contradicts God's word should be discarded, no matter what the author claims.   They are just using God's name in vain. There are false prophets and anti-Christ's among us today, just as the Bible predicts there will be in the last days.   These men are just trying to establish notoriety for themselves, and they usually make a goodly sum of money in the process.

There have been several revised versions of the Bible produced in the last three or four decades.   These attempts at rewriting the Bible have created more controversy than clarification.   I have heard several heated arguments among Christians about which version is the best one.   I myself, (no apologies offered), am guilty of vigorously defending the King James Version (KJV).

While the men who created these modern versions no doubt had honorable intentions, after examining the end product, I have serious doubts that they did this under divine inspiration.   I consider their works to be scholastic rather than spiritual.   There are too many instances where the core idea of a passage, or a group of passages, is radically revised rather than merely simplified.   While I dare not enter into any definitive opinion as to their motives, I can certainly speculate.

Of course, their stated motive in every case was to make the text more understandable to the common man, and in this they have succeeded to a degree. I wholeheartedly believe that was their primary motive, but I feel that there were also other motives, not quite so evident, that governed their works. Perhaps these men were not even consciously cognizant of these motives themselves.

Mankind of late has placed an ever increasing value on intellectual prowess. The wisdom of the past is looked upon as crude and flawed by ignorance. I suspect that at least some of the contributors to these new versions had some degree of doubt in the divine inspiration of the original writers of scripture, considered them intellectually inferior, and therefore considered their works to contain flaws that needed correction. I have three questions for them. Why did God wait so long to bring about these corrections? Has he allowed us to believe in a flawed message from the Bible's creation all the way up to this point? Has mankind finally achieved the intellectual maturity that he is capable of correcting the word of God?

I think that another subtle motive is the unconscious desire to insert denominational doctrines. I know for a fact that if I were to produce a revised version of the Bible, it would lean heavily on Baptist doctrines. I couldn't help myself because that's who I am! (Don't worry, I would never have the audacity, plus, I am completely satisfied with the KJV.)

Probably the most important scripture to all born again believers is John 3:16. The KJV begins this passage with: *For God so loved the world that he gave his only begotten Son-----* In one of the most popular modern versions it reads: *For God so loved the world that he gave his only son*—Why was the word "begotten" omitted?

Once again, I can only speculate. Did the writer not believe in the Immaculate Conception and virgin birth? Was the word purposely omitted because he thought that concept too hard for most people to believe? Or was it merely a "typo" that slipped past the editor's scrutiny?

108

Irregardless of motive, this seems to be a deliberate revision rather than a mere simplification and radically changes the meaning of this passage. Romans 8:14 reads: *For as many as are lead by the spirit of God, they are the sons of God.* Now if Christ is identified in John 3:16 as "his only son", then there is now a direct contradiction between John 3:16 and Romans 8:14. How can those who are led by the spirit be called the sons of God when Christ is his only son? See what happens when man messes with God's holy word?

If we read all of Romans eight, we find that Paul speaks of those who are led by the spirit as being adopted sons so when we read John 3:16 as it was originally written, "only begotten son), there is no more contradiction. Christ was begotten while we were adopted. See, God had it right after all!

I could go on and on through the KJV Bible and the modern versions and point out numerous equally serious cases where man has taken undue liberty with God's word, but I have neither the time nor the patience to list them all, and this book would become one of a set of many volumes, but you can see by the above example that the Bible is best left alone as God gave it.

One other reason that I myself prefer the KJV has nothing to do with my religious beliefs, but I am fond of its literary form. There is a certain lilt and poetic form to the text that is absent in our modern day language versions, that piques my interest and draws my attention.

There are a growing number of people today who are decidedly anti Christianity and would like to see the Bible totally discredited. They actually blame Christianity for many of the ills that plague mankind, and are extremely vocal in their accusations. As the Bible is the basic handbook for Christian living,

Basic
Instructions
Before
Leaving
Earth

they would like nothing better than to see it totally discredited. Organizations like the ACLU and People for the American Way actively participate through the court system in an effort to eradicate all reference to Christianity from the mind of modern man. These groups may make a lot of noise and nibble around the edges, but God's word endures. It endures because it is HIS word and HE is its protector! Try as hard as they will, they can never destroy it.

And worshipped the creature more than the creator

I would describe secular mankind today as generally prideful and arrogant where it concerns his relationship to God. Modern man basks in the limelight, sticks out his chest and says: "I don't need you God, I don't want you God, and look what I have accomplished without you!" I am reminded of the engineer who was the head designer of the Titanic who said: "This boat is so safe, even God couldn't sink her".

Braggadocio is a cantankerous tool, used in an attempt to achieve status that one does not deserve, nor has not earned. The braggart can usually fool those he is attempting to influence, but the success is usually only short lived, and he can never, even for an instant, fool God.

I don't know if God orchestrated the demise of the Titanic because of this man's bragging. I dare not presume to know the workings of God. I can, however, offer justification if he did in fact cause its sinking. It would seem to most people that this would be a horrendous thing for God to sacrifice so many innocent lives just because of one man's bluster. Actually though, there are recorded instances in the Bible where God has sacrificed many more innocent lives than were lost on the Titanic.

First, let's look at the flood in Noah's day. The adults of that era were almost totally corrupt and deserved to die in the flood, but what about the toddlers and babies?

Secondly, when God slew the first born in Egypt, there were children of various ages who were taken in their innocence, and had nothing to do with Pharaoh's mistreatment of the Hebrews. Did they deserve to die for Pharaoh's sins?

Back when I was a new born Christian, and began studying the Bible, I puzzled over these acts of God. I thought, how could he be so cruel? One day I received the answer. Hebrews 9:27 reads *as it is appointed unto man once to die but after this, the judgment.* What difference does it really make if one dies at six years old or at seventy six? Because those young ones were taken in their innocence, they all went to be with the Lord, while if they had grown up to be adults, at least some of them would have turned away from God and been condemned to a fiery hell. That would probably have been a considerable number, due to the totally apostate society in which they would have grown up in. Actually, those were mercifully saved from that condemnation by God's act of judgment.

You might ask "what about the grief of those loved ones that are left behind?" Is the grief of the parents of a deceased six year old any greater than the grief of the children when Mama dies at seventy six? We must all die sometime. I submit that while the circumstances are different the grief and anguish are practically the same in either case.

Let us examine the circumstances that led God to perform these judgments.

The people in Noah's day had become so self centered, proud, and arrogant, that God says of them in Genesis 6:12 *for all flesh had corrupted his way upon the earth. 13. And God said unto Noah, the end of all flesh is come before me; for the earth is filled with violence through them; and, behold, I will destroy them with the earth.* Man's lifestyle had become so godless, that God saw no value in allowing it to continue. (I wonder how close we are to that same point today.)

Pharaoh was mistreating God's chosen people and that is one thing God will not tolerate. I Chronicles 16:22 *saying touch not mine anointed, and do my prophets no harm.* He was touching God's anointed and he paid dearly.

In each of these situations, God was justified in the actions he took. Mankind had gotten "too big for his britches", and refused to submit to the sovereignty of his creator.

Up until a few decades ago, secular mankind passively tolerated the practice of Christianity and in fact, usually considered it a positive influence on societal development. Today, the collective ego of society has become so inflated that man now considers Christianity to be detrimental. He feels that he is more able to shape his own destiny than God is! The destiny that man has chosen for himself is in direct contradiction to God's desire for him.

Modern man has even devised his own religion of sorts, and given it a name: "secular humanism". This has all the attributes of a conventional religion. It has tenets of doctrine, is organized in groups, holds scheduled meetings, and produces literature to expound its beliefs and expand its membership. The only difference between it and religion is that man, (the creature), is held in reverence in place of God, (the creator).

The following is an excerpt from the web page of the Washington area Secular Humanists. I have modified its format to fit this book, but the subtitles and wording are quoted verbatim:

WHAT IS HUMANISM?

Humanism is the contemporary expression of a long tradition of free thought. It is a world view that has inspired many of the world's great thinkers and creative artists.

Humanists believe we can build a better world if we:

Seek *human, rather than divine* (my emphasis) solutions to the world's problems through the application of critical reason, free inquiry and the scientific method.

Continually weigh and test dogmas, ideologies and traditions, whether religious, political or social, against observation, *rather than accepting them on faith.* (once again, my emphasis)

Support democratic forms of government, and affirm the worth, dignity and right to self-determination of every human being.

Maintain the separation of church and state and the freedom of and from religion.

Combine personal liberty with social responsibility, and recognize our dependence on, and responsibility for, the natural world.

<u>Humanists believe we can achieve personal fulfillment through:</u>

A constant search for truth, with the understanding that new knowledge and experience constantly alter our imperfect perception of it.

A concern for this life and a commitment to making it meaningful through better understanding of ourselves, our history, our intellectual and artistic achievements, and the outlook of those who differ from us.

A search for viable individual, social, and political principals of ethical conduct, judging them on their ability to enhance human well being and individual responsibility.

A conviction that with reason, an open market-place of ideas, good will and tolerance, progress can be made in building a better world for ourselves and our children.

(end quote)

One can readily see that humanism is a noble philosophy. A dedicated, practicing humanist would make an exceptional neighbor, friend, or business partner. Some humanists even attend church although if they truly believe their own propaganda, they could not be saved and still be a humanist.

The humanist philosophy is growing by leaps and bounds, as an alternative to religion. It is especially appealing to the modern intellectual because it names man as lord of his own destiny, and of the universe.

Let's look at the statement: "A constant search for truth, with the understanding that new knowledge and experience constantly alter our imperfect perception of it." Pardon me, but isn't truth a constant? Isn't yesterday's truth also today's truth as well as tomorrow's?

While humanism cleverly claims neutrality where religious practice is concerned, it denies that said practice has any purpose in the development of mankind. (See the portions that I have italicized.)

If you read their statement carefully, you can see that they would deny Christianity the right of evangelization, a practice that they themselves partake of. That phrase "freedom of and from religion" is a direct contradiction. If they would give me *freedom of religion*,

113

then I would be duty bound to try to convert them to Christianity, as Christ has specifically instructed me to do, thus violating their "*freedom from religion*".

I am intrigued by the phrase: "A search for viable individual, social, and political principles of ethical conduct" Are we now repealing the Ten Commandments and replacing them by a set of man made rules that are still in the process of formulation? The second part of that phrase: "judging them on their ability to enhance human well being and individual responsibility." Pardon me, but I see nothing about judging them on moral rightness. Picture if you will, the earth surviving for a million more years (extremely unlikely) and the population growth expanding to the point that it would be deemed an "enhancement to human well being" for everyone to be euthanized at age thirty five, due to the overcrowding of the planet. Does that sound fantastic? It fits right in with their statement of belief. Actually, just such a policy was proposed several years ago by a doctor in some medical trade journal where all those elderly who reach age seventy and were incapable of supporting themselves financially or physically would be euthanized rather than become wards of the state. It was just a proposal which no one else supported, but it shows the baseness that man will stoop to when he has no moral compass. I expect that if such a proposal were resubmitted today, it might get some rudimentary consideration in some circles.

To summarize, their creed is basically atheistic, not recognizing the authority of God, or his sovereignty over his creation. While their code of conduct is basically honorable, it is also ungodly. There will be a lot of good practicing, morally correct humanists standing before God on judgment day crying "Why didn't somebody tell me?"

EPILOGUE

WHERE DO WE GO FROM HERE?

If this were a fictional piece, I could skillfully weave the final events into: "they lived happily ever after". Tragically, it is not, I cannot, and they will not!

The depravity of mankind is increasing steadily, and will shortly reach a point where God will personally take control and his awesome judgment will begin.

There are billions of people today who either reject the biblical account of his judgment as fantasy, or consider it to be an event that will occur in the far distant future. For the purpose of explanation, I will examine each of these premises as possibilities, a concept that I soundly reject in each case.

Let us back up to the statement that I made at the end of chapter seven. Quote: A wise man once said:" Man, by his very nature, is destined to strangle in his own physical and moral pollution." End quote. Can you not clearly visualize this twofold pollution alarmingly increasing at the current moment? Given the increases in industrialization and population growth, can you, with any degree of certainty picture mankind ever reversing that trend? I, for one, cannot!

Even if the biblical account is a fantasy, (a concept I refuse to consider), can you not see that man is on a path to self destruction anyway? Not only is the quantity of his self generated pollution increasing, but the rate of increase rises substantially as each year goes by. While man sporadically makes feeble attempts to slow the rate of increase of the physical pollution, he seems to ignore the moral component, in fact, in certain areas, he seems to revel in it. Without a severe moral adjustment, mankind is incapable of reversing the trend, and such adjustment is highly unlikely, if not totally impossible. Instead of recognizing the need to improve his moral conduct, man attempts to push the envelope of his self induced immorality to the very limit. I would compare him to the man who jumped off the Empire State building, and remarked as he passed the tenth floor, "I am OK so far. Modern man sees no need to change; therefore, divine intervention becomes necessary.

Exactly when that point will be reached, only God knows, but be assured, it will happen. Mankind's vehement denial and rebellion demand it. Man has for years attempted to predict the date, but his efforts have been futile. There are, however, certain signs that lead present day Christians who study their Bibles to believe that this final judgment is very near. The arrogant denial of God's sovereignty by modern man is only one of these signs.

There is an embryonic movement of late to develop a world wide system rather than individual nations co-existing on the planet. Pride in ones nation, which was once the mark of a patriot, and considered to be an honorable trait, is now thought of in some circles as bigotry. This new train of thought is on the increase and will eventually result in the emergence of a one world government, to be ruled by the anti-Christ of the book of revelations. This seven year rule will be immediately followed by God's final judgments. In late February or early March of 2009, Prime Minister Gordon Brown of England, in a meeting with President Obama, proposed the establishment of a "global new deal" and the concept of one world currency. While it is probably too early for such ideas to come to fruition, the fact that world leaders are even now discussing them sets a new trend that falls right in with the predictions of the Bible for the end times.

The church of today is gradually losing its power and purity. The standards of behavior and doctrine for the church were established by God in the very beginning of the church age, and the church leaders were held responsible for maintaining those standards. For hundreds of years, those standards were held in sacred trust.

As man began to place more value on development of the intellect than development of the spirit, the popularity of the church waned. In order to maintain its size, status, and popularity, some church leaders took unsanctioned liberty with God's standards. They relaxed them to a more comfortable level, and in some cases to the point that the true God is no longer the object of their worship. The church of today is for the most part in that "lukewarm" state that Christ attributes to the Laodicean church in the book of revelations. In his message to that church he says *"because thou art neither hot nor cold, I will spew thee out of my mouth".* Most churches today have been infiltrated to at least some degree, by godless intellect.

In the book of Mathew, chapter twenty four, the Bible states that in the end times there will be wars and rumors of wars. It is my belief that the current war on terrorism will never end until the beginning of the tribulation. Holy wars in the name of Allah are breaking out all over the globe. As long as there is one radical Muslim left, there will be no surrender. While they realize that there is little hope of establishing a worldwide Islamic theocracy, they will settle for martyrdom as an honorable alternative, and see no need for cessation of hostilities. The more radical Islamists even consider individual martyrdom a victory of sorts. The only one who can end this war is God himself!

The sins of pride, arrogance, greed, and avarice are exponentially on the increase. While I have not seen any surveys on the subject, from my own observations it seems that the number of true Christians per capita today is probably lower than it has ever been at any time since Christianity was born. This coincides with the Biblical prediction that in the latter days there will be a "great falling away".

I previously mentioned the explosion of intelligence that was wrought by the development of the internet. This sudden increase of intelligence is a sign of the end times that was prophesied in the Old Testament.

I am afraid I have not painted a very pretty picture to the intellectual thinker, but the spiritual person should anxiously anticipate these events and take comfort in the fact that the wait will not be long. Luke 21:28 reads *And when these things begin to come to pass, then look up, and lift up your heads; for your redemption draweth nigh.* As a seventy year old man, I am sometimes asked if I would like to go back in time to when I was young; I always reply "No, I'm this close to heaven; I definitely don't want to back up".

Society today is on a slippery slope, heading for self destruction. I fear that what man proudly considers as progress, God sees as digression. As long as mankind remains obsessed with his journey into oblivion, there is little or no chance that he will reverse course. Nothing short of divine intervention will halt his progress, but that is exactly what is coming his way. The cessation of life as we know it has already been envisioned, decreed, and recorded. The real true God, architect of creation, has already sealed the fate of those who continue to rebel, and he has promised eternal reward for the faithful. So be it, Amen.